TUMBLE INTO LOVE

A DIAMOND CREEK, ALASKA NOVEL

J.H. CROIX

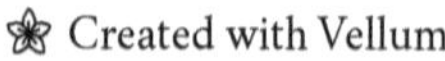 Created with Vellum

To DBC...always.

Sign up for J.H. Croix's newsletter for information on new releases!
http://jhcroixauthor.com/subscribe/

Follow me!
jhcroix@jhcroix.com
https://www.bookbub.com/authors/j-h-croix
https://www.facebook.com/jhcroix
https://www.instagram.com/jhcroix/

*R*isa Holden was driving down the highway from Anchorage to Diamond Creek—a spectacular drive in coastal Alaska with vista after vista of mountains, glaciers, and the ocean unfurling along every mile. She reached the outskirts of Diamond Creek. Her windows were rolled down, and she gloried in the salty ocean air blowing through. She came around a corner to find a moose and two calves ambling across the road. She swerved to avoid them and flinched at the screech as her tires spun out. The guardrail raced toward her, her car hurtled through it, the crunch of steel so loud it hurt her ears. Next came several thumps and a sudden stop when her car bounced into a cluster of alders. Risa sat frozen in her car, stunned and disoriented. There she sat surrounded by alder trees, her car most definitely not going anywhere.

Risa shifted carefully, uncertain if she was injured. It happened so quickly, she hardly had time to think or feel. The alder branches settled around her car. She glanced out her broken window to see a porcupine clinging to a spruce tree nearby, looking curiously in her direction. A stellar jay landed on a branch a few feet away and squawked—as if she'd interrupted the bird's afternoon. Which she supposed she had. Her ears stopped ringing. Her neck felt tight. She tugged the visor down and checked in the mirror. A thin trickle of blood ran down the side of her face. She sifted pieces of broken glass out of her dark hair. Glass was scattered across her lap and throughout the car.

Assessing that she could move, Risa carefully brushed the glass off of her purse and slipped her phone out to call her brother.

Trey answered on the first ring. "Hey sis, when are you due here?"

"Well, I made it to Diamond Creek, but I'm sitting in the middle of a bunch of alder at the bottom of a hill."

After Trey, her overprotective older brother, finished freaking out, he said he'd be on his way as soon as he called 911. He made her promise not to try to get out of her car, which annoyed Risa though she didn't really feel like trying to clamber out. With a sigh, she leaned her head back and wondered how come her life so often felt like it was skidding out of control. Today, it happened to be more than a metaphor.

The sound of sirens carried through the trees. Moments later, footsteps approached her car. She turned and her eyes landed on the sexiest man she'd seen in, well, since she could remember. He had golden brown hair – not quite brown and not quite blond – chocolate brown eyes, and a face an artist would love to paint with sculpted cheekbones, a strong jaw and full, sensual lips. She swore when it occurred to her she must look like hell, what with the blood in her hair and on her face.

To top it off, whoever this amazing man was, he was a cop and looked damn sexy in his uniform. He was clearly built, his shoulders and chest completely filling out his shirt in a mouth-watering way. His eyes held a look of concern when he reached the car. "Hey there, give us a few minutes and we'll get you out of there. Are you hurt?"

Risa sighed. "Aside from the cut on my head, which I can't even see by the way, I think I'm fine. I only stayed put because I promised my brother I would." She moved to open the car door to find it was jammed shut.

Sexy cop moved quickly, bringing his hand against the door. "No, don't do that! I don't want you to accidentally make the roof collapse. It's not looking good from out here, but the door's helping keep it up. I have a crew coming down to get you out safely."

"Okay, okay. I won't move." Risa lifted her hands to show she wasn't trying to open the door anymore. A shiver of fear raced up her spine. Since she felt mostly fine, she'd only stayed put at Trey's insistence. To have sexy cop all worried about her trying to get out was the opposite of comforting at the moment. She swallowed and forced herself to take a slow breath.

"So Trey Holden is your brother?" sexy cop asked.

Risa nodded. "The one and only. Did he call you?"

Sexy cop smiled at her reply. "He did, but I was already on my way out here. Another driver saw the broken guardrail and beat him to it. You must be Risa then."

"Yup. And you are?"

"Darren Thomas. Trey's a friend of mine. Got to know him through Jared Winters who's another friend."

"So you're the wonderful cop who helped dispatch Emma's ex far away from here," Risa said with a grin. Once he said his name, she recognized it. Trey's wife, Emma, had an ex who excelled at being a complete asshole and stalked her for a few years after they broke up. When he showed up in Diamond Creek a while ago, Darren had been instrumental in helping deal with the situation. So he was sexy as hell, her brother's friend, and an upstanding cop who was prone to saving the day, according to Trey at least. On all marks, he was the kind of man a smart woman grabbed onto and never let go. Risa figured he was way too good for her.

Darren lifted an eyebrow at her comment. "Don't know if I'd put it that way, but yes, I helped out with that situation. It's my job."

He turned away at the sound of more footsteps coming through the trees. The next few minutes were a bustle of activity around Risa while she was forced to sit still and repeatedly reminded to do so. The rescue crew was made up of six more men—every single one of them sexy as hell, along with the whole 'I'm here to save you' vibe. While she had her pick of men to stare at, Risa's eyes kept traveling back to Darren as if they were leashed to him.

When they finally pried her door open and she could climb out, she realized how frightened she'd been. She felt shaky once she finally got out of the car

—her heart raced and her legs almost collapsed. She hadn't quite realized how shaken she was until she made an attempt to walk. Fortunately, Darren was right beside her and immediately slipped his arm around her and steadied her.

"Take it easy," he said, his voice a low rumble.

His warm, strong grip was disconcerting. Risa shook her head and tried to shift her weight away, only to stumble again.

"Should've known you'd be stubborn like your brother," Darren said with a soft chuckle. He glanced over to the cluster of men. "We need to get her up to the ambulance. Can one of you get on her other side and help me walk her up the hill?"

One of the guys nodded, while another asked if they needed to get a stretcher for her.

"I can walk. I'm fine!" Risa declared.

Darren ignored her. "I don't think she needs a stretcher. She's just not too steady on her feet." He looked down at her, those amazing brown eyes colliding with hers. "You probably are fine, but I'm not taking any chances. Trey'll kick my ass if I do."

"I don't answer to my brother, so don't go thinking you need to on my behalf."

Darren's lips quirked and he shrugged. "In this case, I do, so you'll have to deal with it."

Risa felt disconcertingly pleased to have Darren insist on taking care of her, though she should have been annoyed. Darren looked away when one of the men approached them. "Risa, this is Travis," he said tipping his head in Travis's direction.

Travis had light brown hair and blue eyes. He nodded and smiled. "Glad you're doing okay.

Could've been much worse. Your car is totaled though."

Risa turned to look at her car—a trusty, old blue hatchback. It had taken her many places, but it was clearly done with that now, its roof crumpled and the front end bent entirely out of shape. She looked back at Travis with a sigh. "I know," she said ruefully. "Nice to meet you."

With a quick grin, he moved to the side of her opposite from Darren. Without a word, he slipped his arm under her shoulder and nodded to Darren. With most of her weight borne by them, she made her way up the hill. Though Travis was handsome, objectively speaking, and he was draped around her as well, she didn't feel the slightest spark with him. Darren's closeness, on the other hand, was disturbingly distracting. She was startled at how easily he affected her. Usually, she could appreciate a man's looks without turning into a puddle.

When they reached the road, Trey's car was pulling up behind the ambulance. He raced to her side with his wife, Emma, following at a slower pace. "Are you okay?" Trey asked the second he reached her.

"Trey, I'm fine. You'll be happy to know Darren wouldn't let me get out of the car by myself and insisted on having Travis help him walk me up the hill," Risa replied wryly.

Trey looked to Darren. "Thanks man. I know how stubborn Risa can be, so I appreciate you being here."

Risa rolled her eyes and went to move away from Darren and Travis though neither budged. "Um, guys?"

"Let's get you seated over there," Travis said, gesturing toward the back of the ambulance.

Risa realized she was surrounded by men who thought they knew best, so she elected not to argue the point and quietly made her way over to the back of the ambulance.

When Darren finally stepped away, she instantly missed his warm strength. A friendly female emergency responder greeted her and quickly checked her over. In short order, the cut near her hairline had been cleaned and bandaged. After a quick overall check and a run of tests to assess whether she had a concussion, they determined she didn't need stitches and cleared her to leave. Trey stood with Darren and Travis talking.

Risa glanced to Emma who'd joined her by the ambulance. "You look amazing, as usual. I still can't believe you had a baby a few months ago. How's Janet?" Risa asked with a smile.

Emma grinned at the name of her months-old baby. "She's great. When you called, Hannah was at the house, so she stayed with Janet while we came to get you." Her eyes coasted over Risa. "Great entrance today. Ready to head to our place?"

Risa nodded and stood carefully. Trey approached them in the road. "I wasn't thinking when we left. The back of the car is a mess with the car seat and some of my fishing gear."

Darren was right on Trey's heels. "Risa can ride with me. I'll follow you to your place," he offered. Risa's pulse leapt at his words with her mind instantly trying to point out she was being ridiculous.

Trey turned to Darren. "You sure you don't mind?"

Darren shook his head. Trey looked to her. "Do you mind riding with Darren?"

Risa did and didn't. If it weren't for the fact that

the electricity crackling between them was a force to be reckoned with, she wouldn't mind at all. She couldn't come up with a rational reason to say no, so she merely shrugged and followed Darren to his patrol car.

The car was quiet as Darren drove. They'd been delayed for a few minutes after Trey and Emma left when Darren was called over to respond to some questions from the tow truck guy. Since it was a single vehicle accident, it had been quickly decided that Risa's car would be dragged back up the hill and towed to the local junkyard where it would await the insurance assessor who would likely determine the vehicle totaled in less than one minute. Risa had called Trey to let him know she'd be there once Darren finished up.

She glanced around Darren's patrol car. Aside from the radio and the divider between the front and back, it was rather basic. She wasn't accustomed to sitting on a bench seat without a console. Her mind couldn't help but think how easy it would be to slide right over and soak up the warmth she knew emanated from Darren.

Darren came to a stop at a stoplight and glanced over at her. She wanted to dive into his eyes and wished he wasn't her brother's friend. Before she'd discovered that inconvenient detail, she'd been thinking a little fling would be perfect. Trey was friends with half the town practically. As these thoughts tumbled through her mind, she realized she was staring at Darren, and he was staring right back. Desire coursed through her. A horn honked behind them.

Darren tore his eyes from hers and turned away,

driving through the light. She wanted to draw his profile. The lines of his face were beautiful and strong. He had a faint scar on the side of his face. Close to his ear, it traced a faded path up to his temple and into his hair—that honey brown hair she wanted to run her fingers through.

Risa forced herself to look away and wondered if she'd lost her mind. She didn't know what it was about this man, but his body and hers seemed to be having a conversation over which she had no control. Her pulse raced, her breath was shallow and heat slid through her.

"So how often do you come down to Diamond Creek?"

Darren's voice was deep and steady. His question was so benign, her thoughts the second before embarrassed her.

"I try to get down here once a month. I live in Anchorage."

Darren nodded. "Yeah, Trey mentioned that. I grew up there."

Her curiosity was piqued. "You did? What brought you to Diamond Creek?"

Darren glanced at her, his eyes warm. She could have sworn they fell to her breasts and back up, but it was so fast, she couldn't be sure.

"Oh, I moved away from Anchorage when I went to college down in Washington. I came to Diamond Creek when I got offered a job here. I was done with the whole urban cop beat after Seattle, so Diamond Creek got me back to Alaska and a much slower pace. I love it here," he said.

He had to stop again at the light in the intersection that would bring them up the hill toward Trey's house. He looked over at her. She was so flustered, she didn't know where to look, but she couldn't look away. She was beginning to wonder if she'd hit her head harder than she thought in the accident.

When the light changed, Darren turned up the road and abruptly turned again onto an unfamiliar road. Before Risa could ask where they were going, he pulled into a driveway surrounded by trees. He stopped the car quickly and looked at her again. The electricity humming between them arced higher.

Risa's eyes were locked into the heat of his chocolate gaze. Her pulse was off the charts.

"I think I've lost my mind, but I have to kiss you. You say the word, and I'll turn around and drive you right to Trey's place." Darren's eyes held hers.

She couldn't have told him to turn around if her life depended on it. Instead, she slid across that handy bench seat and paused inches away from him. He lifted his hand and brushed a loose tendril of hair out of her eyes, his fingers sliding around her ear, shivers following. Never breaking eye contact, he slowly lowered his head until his lips met hers.

The first touch of his lips was soft—almost a question. The answer was a shock of sensation racing through her body, heat unfurling in a wave. She slid her hand behind his head, through the soft layers of his hair, and tugged him close. Her mouth fell open and she dove into the most intense, devouring kiss she'd ever experienced. He traced her lips with his tongue, delving in with deep strokes, their tongues tangling. She pulled away to catch her breath. His lips blazed a heated trail down her neck. Her breath came in gusts against his hair. Hot shivers skated across her skin and she shifted to get closer.

Suddenly, Darren pulled back. "We have to slow down," he whispered.

Risa realized she was half in his lap. Her thoughts were a jumble. She looked into his eyes. Strangely, she felt like she'd known him for far, far longer than she had. The haze of passion began to clear in her mind. Whatever this was between them was a bit…too much. She carefully pulled away, her body protesting.

"Well," she said, her voice thick with feeling. "I, uh…"

"Don't know what the hell this is?" Darren offered helpfully.

She looked over at him, his eyes mirroring her uncertainty and dazed feeling. As startled and confused as she was, she felt an instant comfort with him. His eyes crinkled at the corners with his grin. She laughed and nodded. "Definitely not."

Darren's palm had been on her back when she shifted away and it remained there, a warm anchor.

CHAPTER 2

*D*arren strode into his office, kicking the door shut behind him. Seconds later, there was a quick knock and the door opened again. Sylvia Cunningham stood there with her arms crossed. Sylvia's official title was administrative assistant, but she was affectionately known as the center of the universe at the station. Her husband Michael had retired as police chief over five years ago. She'd pretty much run the show with him for decades in Diamond Creek. Diamond Creek was much bigger now and growing every year, but back when Michael started as police chief, Sylvia had done her role on a volunteer basis for years, handling everything from dispatch to filing to occasionally dealing with unruly prisoners. During her thirty years here, she'd gone from being a volunteer to paid staff while the police force had grown from a one-man show to ten officers.

Michael had hired Darren to take his place when a back injury made continuing to work as a cop near to impossible. He'd reluctantly retired, but still checked in at the station several times a week. Sylvia's appearance belied her steely nature. She barely topped five feet and had a cozy, motherly vibe. She was round and soft with bright blue eyes and white hair that bounced in a curly bob. Pretty much nothing intimidated her, and she was one of the kindest, most no-nonsense people Darren had ever known.

At the moment, she looked perturbed.

"Good morning, Sylvia. You've got a look. What did I do?" he asked.

Sylvia's eyes twinkled, but she pursed her lips. "You forgot to put your reports in my office last night. Now I'm behind on data entry." She sighed and tapped her foot.

Sylvia was trying her damnedest to get Darren to rely on her more for things like entering his reports in the system, but old habits died hard. Darren had come here from Seattle where administrative support was stretched so thin, he did as much as he could himself. After every other approach failed, Sylvia's new tactic was to guilt him into it.

Darren reached for the stack of reports tucked beside his computer. He handed them to her with flourish. "I take a while to train. I'm working on it," he replied with a grin.

"Did you get a cup of coffee yet?" Sylvia asked once she had the reports in hand.

"No, I..."

Darren was speaking to thin air. Sylvia had whirled out of his office. He chuckled and followed her to the break room. "Sylvia, you don't need to wait on me," he said as he caught up to her.

She turned away from the coffee pot and handed him a cup of coffee. "How about you add cream?"

Darren shook his head. After he'd added a dash of cream, he took a welcome sip of coffee. Travis Wilkes strode into the break room at that moment. The building that housed the police station was connected to the fire station though their entrances were on parallel streets. They shared a break room and storage in the connector between the buildings. Travis was a firefighter, emergency responder and fisherman. Like most Alaskans, he was jack of multiple trades. While Darren was mostly a cop, he was also a fisherman and did back up duty as a backcountry firefighter.

"Hey man, how's it going today?" Travis asked, running a hand through his hair.

Darren shrugged and glanced at his watch. "It's seven in the morning. So far, so good. Here's hoping today's quieter than yesterday."

Sylvia beat Travis to the coffee pot as well and quickly served him a cup. Travis grinned and pecked her on the cheek. He looked back to Darren. "Yeah, yesterday had us running all over. Between the car accident and the fires up on the hill, I didn't get home last night 'til after ten." He paused and took a sip of coffee, his blue eyes taking on a glint of mischief. "So it was nice of you to offer to take Risa home yesterday."

Darren should have seen that coming. Travis was sharp and noticed everything. He also loved to tease. Sylvia had started to walk out of the break room and immediately turned, looking expectantly at Darren.

Darren shrugged. "She needed a ride. Why wouldn't I offer her one?"

"Of course. Makes perfect sense. It wasn't so much the ride as the fact that you couldn't keep your eyes off of her," Travis said with a chuckle before spinning on his heel and leaving through the door into the fire station.

Heat crept up his neck, but Darren ignored it. He glanced toward Sylvia who lifted an eyebrow.

"Sylvia, I offered a woman a ride after she had a car accident. Not exactly gossip."

"That you paid enough attention to a woman that anyone notices *is* gossip," she replied archly. Her eyes softened as she studied him. "It wouldn't hurt you to find someone. You've got a heart of gold," she said softly. She took a step and squeezed his arm before turning and walking away quietly.

The mere mention of Risa conjured her in Darren's mind. When he'd walked down the short hill to find her car pinned in the trees yesterday, he'd been worried about whoever was in the car. The moment he saw her, he'd had to force himself to stay focused. She'd turned those dark brown eyes on him, and he could hardly look away. Her deep, rich brown hair was a messy bob, glinted with pieces of glass that she'd been combing out when he approached. Her lips were full and deep red, a contrast to her dark hair and eyes. Her wry smile held a hint of vulnerability underneath.

If he were being honest with himself, he would have to admit he'd leapt at the chance to offer her a ride to her brother's house. Then he'd completely lost his mind. He'd never laid eyes on a woman and felt the kind of pull he did to Risa. His body had hijacked his brain when he turned off the main road and pulled into his own driveway. He simply couldn't let her out of his sight without kissing her first. And damn if that kiss didn't make matters worse. He'd managed to get himself under control and stop, but he couldn't even walk into Trey's house when he dropped her off for fear it would be obvious to everyone that he had a raging hard on. He felt a twinge of guilt thinking about the fact that Trey's sister got him so hot, he could hardly think straight. Trey probably wouldn't like to know Darren had to take a cold shower when he got home after kissing Risa.

Darren realized he was standing by himself in middle of the break room. He swore and walked briskly to his office, kicking the door shut behind him again. With a sigh, he sat at his desk, running a hand through his hair and clicking his computer on. He absently fingered the scar that ran along the side of his face into his hairline.

CHAPTER 3

Risa walked into the kitchen at Trey and Emma's house. Her knees almost gave out when a small body hurtled against her legs from behind. "Aunt Risa!"

She leaned down, meeting her nephew's eyes upside down. "Hey Stu, what's up?" she asked with a grin.

Stuart, her favorite and only nephew, giggled and released her legs. She grabbed him, lifting him for a hug. "You're getting so big! I can barely pick you up anymore!"

Stuart wiggled, and she set him down, ruffling his brown hair, which had tufts sticking up all over. He grinned at her with those eyes, so like her brother's, soft brown with gold flecks. He quickly turned away and ran to the kitchen table, sliding into a chair.

"Mom's in the shower. I'm 'sposed to tell you there's coffee ready."

Risa had already made it to the kitchen to find Emma had set a mug out for her by the coffee pot. She filled it and joined Stuart at the table. "Your mom knows how much I like my morning coffee. So where's your little sister?"

Stuart smiled widely. He'd had a few weeks of jealousy after Janet was born three months ago, but he'd adjusted and was now a very proud older brother. "Dad took her to his office so Lucy could see her." He paused to sift his fingers through Tootsie's hair when he twined around Stuart's chair, purring madly. Tootsie was the orange tabby cat Risa had given to Stuart in the months after his mother died. That had been a rough and heart-wrenching time for Trey and Stuart. Helen, Trey's first wife and Stuart's birth mother, had died unexpectedly from an undiagnosed heart defect over four years ago now. Risa had wanted Stuart to have someone to comfort him. Tootsie seemed perfect, and he'd turned out to be the best kind of cat for a little boy. He was patient, tolerant and slept with Stuart every night.

Risa hadn't stopped worrying about Trey and Stuart until Emma came along though. It had been hard to watch how the loss of Helen affected them. Trey was the kind of man who wanted to share his life with someone and whose grief had been deepened by witnessing his young son try to cope with the loss of his mother. Though they had moved on by the time Trey met Emma, Emma had brought the sun back into their lives. Risa sipped her coffee and smiled at that.

"Does your head hurt?" Stuart asked, pointing to the small bandage on her forehead.

Risa shook her head. "Not really." She fingered the bandage, experiencing only residual soreness from the cut underneath. Thinking back to the accident, she realized she was quite lucky. Fortunately, alder trees were quite the bramble and slowed her car significantly on its way down the short hill. Trey had pointed out the alders had essentially served as a net for her car.

Thinking about her accident instantly brought Darren to mind, which flushed her straight through. She'd fallen asleep last night replaying his kiss. Desire coursed through her, and she shook her head. Now was definitely not the time and place for daydreams about the sexiest man she'd ever met.

Emma walked into the living room and toward the kitchen. "Morning," she said, pausing by Risa's chair to squeeze her shoulder.

"Hey there, thanks for getting coffee ready for me."

"I'd like to say it was just for you, but I can't get through the first hour of the day without coffee. So you're welcome," Emma replied with a grin as she filled her own mug and joined them at the table.

"Stu, did Dad tell you what time he'd be back?" Emma asked.

Stuart looked at the clock. "I think he said around eleven. Am I going to nature school today?"

Emma nodded. "That's the plan. Landon will be there too. His mom told me when I saw her yesterday."

Stuart's eyes lit up, and he leapt from his chair. "When can we go?"

Emma grinned. "As soon as you're ready."

Stuart barreled down the hall to his room.

Emma turned to Risa. Emma was flat beautiful—tall and curvy with long dark hair and bright blue eyes. But with Emma, it wasn't her looks that mattered. She was warm and kind and made Trey's small family whole again. Risa adored her.

"Want to go with me while I drop Stuart off? We could stop and grab lunch somewhere."

"Sounds good to me."

A bit later, Risa walked alongside Emma into The Boatyard Café, a restaurant situated on a bluff overlooking Kachemak Bay. It was an updated diner with delicious food. They barely managed to beat the lunch rush, snagging a booth moments before a line formed at the entrance. Not long after they ordered, Susie Hammond, a friend of Emma's, approached the booth.

Susie was quite obviously pregnant. She slipped into the booth with a sigh. "Hey girls, it's a tight fit, but I made it," she said with a grin. She turned to Emma. "Just so you know, I hate how tall you are."

Emma rolled her eyes and shrugged. "I refuse to apologize for my height."

Susie sighed and tucked her wild brown curls behind her ears. "You and Hannah made it look easy to be pregnant. I've discovered being five feet tall and pregnant is very different. There's nowhere for my weight to go, but out. I feel like a beach ball. I cannot wait for this to be over!"

Emma chuckled. "Aren't you due next week?"

Susie nodded vigorously, her brown eyes lighting up. "Yes!" She turned to Risa. "Hey Risa, how's it going? I heard you made quite the entrance yesterday," she said with a grin.

Their waitress stopped by to take Susie's order. Risa waited until she was gone before speaking. "You could say that again. I swerved to avoid a moose and her babies and ended up going through the guardrail on the hill coming into town. My car's totaled, but aside from this cut," she gestured to her forehead "I'm doing okay."

"It could've been much worse, I'm just glad you're okay," Emma commented before leaning back when the waitress brought their sandwiches.

"How are they getting your car out of there?" Susie asked.

"Darren said the tow crew would hook it to a pulley and drag it up the hill. Now I have to deal with the whole insurance thing and find a new car," Risa replied with a sigh.

"Darren is such a good guy," Susie said.

"I still can't believe that man's managed to stay single, nice as he is," Emma commented before taking a bite of her sandwich.

"I know. Maybe it's time for me to set him up," Susie said thoughtfully.

Emma burst out laughing and shook her head. "It's a wonder you're an accountant. You clearly missed your calling. What if Darren doesn't want to be set up?"

Susie shrugged. "According to Sylvia...you know the old chief's wife who still works there?" At Emma's nod, she continued. "She says he's gun shy. Something about how he got hurt back when he was a cop in Seattle."

Risa's mind whirred. Just thinking about Darren got her pulse going. She was dying to ask about him, but that would guarantee too many nosy questions from Emma and Susie, so she kept quiet. Susie and Emma chatted about work, and Risa focused on eating.

"So Risa, how come you don't move down to Diamond Creek?" Susie asked suddenly.

Risa shrugged. "I hadn't really thought about it." As soon as she answered, she wondered why she hadn't. She'd stayed in Anchorage mostly out of habit. She and Trey had grown up there. After she'd attended college in Juneau, she'd returned to Anchorage and eventually found work managing an art gallery. She loved painting and while it didn't pay the bills, the added income from managing the gallery kept her afloat.

Risa looked back at Susie. "You have a point. Maybe I should move here." She looked between Emma and Susie. "Honestly, the only reason I've stayed in Anchorage is because I love my job. If I thought there was any chance of finding something like that down here, I'd seriously think about it."

Emma was mid-chew on a bite of her sandwich, but she grinned widely and lifted her hand for a high five.

Susie gave her a satisfied smile. "Guess I should have suggested that sooner. I was thinking it's nice to see you every month or so, but it would be even better if you were here all the time. I figured you stayed there because of...what's your boyfriend's name again?"

Risa's stomach felt hollow. She hadn't told Trey and Emma about the mortifying end to her most recent relationship even though it had been months since it ended. She'd met Brad at the art gallery she managed. He ran another local art gallery. He'd been funny, charming and handsome. They'd started dating, and Risa thought perhaps she'd finally met a man she could bring home to meet her family.

While Trey was the model son, following their father's footsteps into the Air Force and getting his law degree, she was the misfit in her family. After rising in the ranks of the Air Force, their father had gone on to start a law practice outside of Anchorage and was later appointed as a judge. Their mother had been an English professor first at a small college in Seattle and then later at the University of Alaska. Risa had no trouble academically, but it bored her silly. She scraped through college by a hair and the only time she felt interested and motivated was when she was painting.

As for her love life, it consisted of casual relationships that went nowhere. At thirty-one, she knew her parents expected her to settle down with someone in the near future. It wasn't that she didn't want to, but she hadn't found anyone who made her feel good enough to stay in the relationship. Along came Brad who owned and ran his own art gallery and seemed on the surface to be a good guy. Little did she know that he was having a side fling with her friend Gretchen for most of their relationship. Risa had become friends with Gretchen through a painting group. She'd discovered Brad and Gretchen's relationship when she'd stopped to pick up takeout one night after work. She'd believed Brad to be out of town. It was mid-winter and dark outside. They were sitting thigh to thigh at a table by the window of an adjacent restaurant with Brad kissing his way down Gretchen's neck.

Risa was nothing if not direct. She'd walked into the restaurant and stopped by their table to return Brad's house key and demanded he return hers immediately. It was the first time his façade fell. He was flustered and angry. Gretchen had babbled all kinds of excuses. Risa hadn't spoken to either one of them since.

"I didn't realize that was a loaded question," Susie commented bluntly.

Risa flushed when she realized she'd been silent for a bit too long. With a bitter smile, she replied, "There is no boyfriend. Which makes it all the more sensible to think about getting the hell out of Anchorage. But before I do that, I have to find a job here."

Emma turned to her, her eyes worried. "What happened to Brad?"

Risa shook her head. "He turned out to be a jerk." She turned to Susie. "So what are my chances for finding decent work here?"

"Well, Diamond Creek isn't Anchorage, but we have plenty of galleries with the flood of tourists every summer. It's probably an issue of timing. Summer's winding down soon here, so you'd be more likely to find work next spring. What do you think, Emma?" Susie asked, turning to her.

Emma's blue eyes landed on Risa. "You can figure out the work thing if you want to be here. You might not score a job as good as the one you have now, but if you're willing to be flexible, you'll eventually find something you're happy with. It's like going anywhere new, you have to get the lay of the land and wait and see. You know you can stay with us. We'd would love it if you were here."

"I can't plan to stay with you guys as a long-term thing. I'll need to feel like I'm here on my terms, not just mooching off of you."

Emma shook her head. "Risa, you've always been there for us. Staying with us until you sort out where you live is perfectly fine. But that's not what you're worried about. I wish you realized it's okay to ask for help and rely on people who love you."

Emma's comment hit home, and Risa started to feel defensive when Susie spoke. "Join the club," she said, catching Risa's eyes with a wry grin. "I love helping everyone and can't stand feeling like I might need somebody's help. It's a true affliction." Susie turned to Emma. "You're the therapist. How do we make this go away? It's even worse when people notice it," she said pointedly.

Emma grinned. Her gaze sobered when she looked to Risa again. "I didn't mean to make you uncomfortable. If we're being honest, I can be just as bad as the two of you, and you both know it. So..." her eyes lightened again "...my point is, regardless of where you stay, I bet you can find work at a local gallery, one way or another. We'd love it if you were here full-time."

As they drove away, Risa pondered her resistance to relying on friends and family. If she could chalk it up to anything, it was that she felt like she needed to prove she could do things herself. After drifting along aimlessly for longer than she thought she should've, she was proud of her work managing the gallery in Anchorage. She loved her bosses, and didn't want to lose something that made her feel good. But aside from her job, there was nothing holding her in Anchorage. Her parents lived nearby, but she tended to visit with them every few weeks, which she could easily do if she lived in Diamond Creek. Darren flitted in the corner of her thoughts. *You cannot be thinking about moving here because you have the hots for a man you just met. He's a side benefit. I have plenty of other reasons to move here. Yeah, but you only considered it seriously after you practically lost your mind over him.* She laughed when she realized she was arguing with herself. But thinking about Darren did send heat sliding through her veins. The idea that she could be near him on a regular basis was tempting to say the least.

Later that afternoon, Risa pulled up at Red Truck Coffee, an outdoor coffee stop housed in an old bread truck painted bright red. It was situated by the harbor, which led to an endless stream of business. Emma had let Risa borrow one of their cars for the afternoon. After she got a cup of her favorite coffee and weaved her way through the tourists milling around the relentlessly busy coffee stop, she heard her name. Her heart immediately stuttered and raced.

She turned to find Darren leaning against his patrol car, which was parked beside Emma's car. He was just as sexy as she'd recalled last night when she fantasized about him. She flushed remembering how hot and bothered she'd been after their kiss yesterday.

"Hey," she said.

Darren smiled, those sensual lips quirking higher on one side. "Hey there. How're you feeling today?" he asked, gesturing to her forehead.

"Oh, just fine. My neck's a little sore, but that's it."

He nodded. She stood in front of him, frozen and unable to think clearly. His chocolate gaze pinned her in place. He looked so damn sexy in his uniform. She'd never considered herself to be into uniforms, but on Darren...oh dear god. He looked delicious and authoritative.

After a long silence, he spoke again. "How long will you be in town?"

Risa shrugged. "Now that I don't have a car, I'm not so sure. I'm also thinking about moving down here. Maybe now's the time to do it." She couldn't believe she'd told him that, but the mere sight of him made her want to confide in him.

Darren's eyes took a gleam, but he merely nodded at her comment. After another long silence, he took a deep breath. "I was wondering if I could take you out to dinner," he said, the words stilted. A muscle ticked in his jaw. His eyes were carefully guarded.

Risa thought about the tiny nugget of information Susie dropped—that he was gun shy about relationships—and wondered what lay behind it. He exuded calm and strength. The idea that he might have been hurt by someone made her curious. She wanted to know and to make it better. She didn't know how she could know, seeing as she barely knew him, but she sensed he was a good man. But then her judgment wasn't so great in that area, seeing as she'd thought Brad was a good man. Nevertheless, the vague idea that someone had hurt Darren and led him to keep to himself made her want to know how...and to climb through his defenses.

Though every ounce of logic in her cautioned against opening herself up to anyone, she wanted Darren with a ferocity hard to resist. Logic lost. "I'd like that," she replied carefully. "When?"

Darren looked startled at her reply, almost as if he'd expected her to say no. He flushed, which relieved Risa because she didn't want to be the only one feeling ridiculous. "How about tomorrow night?"

"Perfect. Name the place and I'll meet you there." As soon as the words left her mouth, she remembered she didn't have a car. "Scratch that. Can you pick me up?"

Darren grinned and nodded. "Any favorites in town?"

"Nope. You decide. I'll give you my number and you can text me. Just tell me what time you'll come by to pick me up." She quickly recited her number to him while he tapped it into his phone.

They were interrupted by a man who cuffed Darren on the back and proceeded to launch into a discussion on whether or not the town should add another stoplight at one of the intersections that clogged with traffic every summer.

Darren's radio went off once the man walked away. He glanced apologetically at Risa. "Sorry about that. I'm gonna have to take off."

"Do I get your number too?" she asked. She felt like a schoolgirl, silly and flushed.

Darren gave her his number before climbing back in his car. Risa desperately wanted to kiss him, but she barely knew him. If she dared to do so, the gossip would race like brushfire. Instead, she smiled and waved as he drove away, willing her pulse to slow down.

CHAPTER 4

ive years ago

Darren's police radio blared, reporting an accident on I-5, one of the busiest high-ways flowing through Seattle. He was less than a minute from the location of the accident. He switched his siren on and zoomed through traffic, arriving first on the scene. As he pulled up behind the two-vehicle accident, he quickly realized one vehicle was in much worse shape than the other. A small sedan was crumpled against the guardrail, pinned between the guardrail and the other vehicle, which had come to a rest against the driver side door.

Darren ran to check on the passengers. There were two people waiting beside the car on the outside who appeared to be banged up, but okay enough to have gotten themselves out. One of them, a young woman, was crying so hard she was hyperventilating. Darren followed her eyes to the other car and saw a toddler boy strapped into a car seat, glass scattered across him with blood running down his cheek. He looked stunned. As Darren's eyes absorbed the scene, he saw that the two adults in the front were unconscious. If the man who had been driving were still alive, Darren would be amazed. The car door was crushed into him, and he was collapsed over the steering wheel.

The hood of the car had smoke billowing out of it. Sirens could be heard in the distance, but definitely not close enough that Darren could wait for more help to arrive. As he scrambled to reach the car, he radioed an update. The following minutes seared into his brain. He remembered choking fear when he reached the car and realized he couldn't easily get the little boy out. He smashed away the remnants of the window and frantically reached through. It felt like a miracle almost happened when he got the little boy unbuckled from the car seat. Then, he heard a voice yelling his name and the car exploded in flames.

* * *

Present day

Darren came awake abruptly, fear pounding through him. Sweat covered his body. He threw the sheets off and swore. A glance at the clock told him it was three in the morning. With a sigh, he got up and walked to the shower. Whenever he dreamt about the accident, the only thing that calmed him was to take a shower. As the steaming water coasted over his body, he wondered if it would help if he remembered anything else from that day. Somehow, he doubted it. The dream contained his entire memory, ending right when the car was engulfed in fire. His memory was blank from that point until the next day when he woke in the hospital and his unit sergeant carefully told him that the little boy had died in the fire.

Darren had inhaled a massive gulp of hot smoke, which scorched his lungs, and had sustained an injury on the side of his face, believed to have occurred when he leaned through the window to reach for the little boy. He was hospitalized until his lungs recovered. All that remained of the accident was the faint scar running in a jagged line from his cheek into his hairline above his ear...and nightmares.

Not long after, he'd started searching for a job in Alaska. He couldn't bear to drive past the site of the accident for months. When he finally managed to drive by, cold dread rolled over him every time. The psychologist his job sent him to explained what Darren was experiencing was normal, the aftereffects of a traumatic event. Darren did everything the psychologist suggested, and the superficial symptoms improved. He could drive down the highway without wanting to vomit, he could do his job without his adrenaline pumping on high all day, he could see toddlers and not envision the little boy in that car, but he didn't want to be in Seattle anymore. All he knew was he wanted to go home. He'd applied for the police chief position in Diamond Creek, thinking it was a long shot. He'd figured it would go to someone local. When he'd met with Michael Cunningham, he'd felt instantly comfortable. Michael offered him the job within a week of the interview, explaining he needed someone in the position before he stepped down as chief.

Darren climbed back in bed after his shower, staring at the stars through the skylight window directly above his bed. Risa strolled into his thoughts.

Her dark hair was a tousled bob, her eyes sharp and probing, and her lips...well, they were so damn kissable, he'd had to force himself not to kiss her when he saw her yesterday at the coffee place by the harbor. He hadn't been as alone as Sylvia at work imagined him to be, but he hadn't had a relationship either. He kept things light and didn't see anyone local. Too many potential complications. He found company when he traveled, which was usually a few times a month for work. Ever since the accident that haunted his dreams, he couldn't imagine trying to have a relationship. How would he explain his nightmares? He knew without question, if Risa got close enough to know him and see him when he woke like this during the night, she'd think he was broken. He couldn't bear that.

RISA SAT beside Stuart on the couch with Tootsie napping between them. Stuart was engrossed in looking at a plant magazine while Risa clicked through job ads on her laptop. Susie's question and their subsequent discussion about living here had mobilized her. Her phone bleeped, indicating a text had arrived. Darren's name was on the banner that bounced on her screen.

Still up for dinner?
Of course!
Diamond Creek Brewery? 6pm?
Perfect. Don't forget I'll need a ride.
No problem. Pick you up at Trey's place?
Where else would I be?
Um...don't know. Just checking.

. . .

RISA SET HER PHONE DOWN, her stomach fluttering. She couldn't quite believe she was about to have dinner with Darren and wondered if she'd completely lost her mind. He was way too sexy and way too good for her. *So you'll just have a fling. Don't make this more than it is. He's hot. You haven't had good sex in pretty much forever. Just have fun.* Risa shook her head sharply, knocking her thoughts away. Maybe she was crazy, but Darren spoke to her body in a way no one had. She wouldn't worry about getting intimate and would ignore the lingering fear he might not be what he seemed. It wouldn't matter if she didn't let things get too serious. *It's not just that. You're afraid you're not good enough for him.* Risa swore to herself. She didn't need to think about that. She'd simply enjoy the smoking hot chemistry between them. She contemplated what she would tell Trey when he asked about Darren and decided to take the friend angle if he asked.

A few hours later, Risa rode in Darren's car toward town. She'd gotten lucky with Trey still finishing up at work when Darren arrived to pick her up. Emma had merely nodded when she'd told her she was having dinner with a friend. Risa had a few local friends that she often spent time with when she came to visit, so she'd made sure to slip out the door as soon as Darren pulled up.

The mere act of sitting in the car with Darren had her pulse racing and her breath shallow. Out of uniform, Darren was even more handsome. He wore jeans that hugged his muscled legs and a t-shirt that molded over his muscled chest and arms. Risa's hands itched to touch him. The level of chemistry between them reinforced her plan to keep this casual. She wasn't ready to tangle with what it meant to let someone matter again, especially not when the chemistry between them made her body hum to the special tune he evoked. If that happened, she'd have to face her doubts that he could be like Brad. Or worse, he wouldn't be like Brad, and she'd somehow have to live up to that. A tiny corner of her mind pointed out she might be biting off more than she could chew.

Diamond Creek Brewery was bustling. Darren had wisely called ahead to make reservations, and they were quickly escorted through the crowd in the entryway to a booth. Risa loved this restaurant. Good food, funky atmosphere and an amazing view of Kachemak Bay and the mountains in the distance. The restaurant was in an old plane hangar, refurbished and decorated with bright colors and model planes artfully hanging from the ceiling. The booths were fairly private, and the noise muffled once they were seated.

Darren looked over at her, his eyes simmering with banked heat. She'd always thought brown eyes were rather plain, or that's what she thought about her own. On Darren, they were a study in subtle contrasts. His were alternately warm and soft and hot and dark. His velvet gaze elicited a spark of heat every time he looked her way. She sipped her wine and tried to get a hold of herself.

"So you said you used to live in Seattle?" she asked, trying for a neutral topic.

"Yup. After college, I went to the police academy there and started on the force once I was done."

"And you came to Diamond Creek because…?"

For a split second, Risa saw a flash of deep pain in Darren's eyes. He masked it so quickly, she thought she must have imagined it.

"I missed Alaska and I was ready for a change of pace. The chief position was up for hire here, so I applied. I'd been to Diamond Creek before. My parents used to bring us fishing in the summer, and I knew it was a great place."

"Didn't you say the other day you were thinking of moving here?" His return question threw her off, mostly because she didn't know precisely what she wanted. She only knew her life in Anchorage made her feel restless and her blow up with Brad had narrowed her friend circle. Gretchen had been one of her closer friends in the painting world, and Brad's role as a gallery owner threw her in his path more frequently than she preferred. Risa was over Brad, but she wasn't over the recognition that she had damn poor judgment.

She realized she had yet to answer Darren. "Yeah, I'm thinking about it. I don't have much keeping me in Anchorage. I'm close to Trey and Emma, and it'd be nice to be around more often for my nephew and niece."

Darren nodded politely. As dinner continued, Risa found herself torn. Her head wanted to keep this light and casual, while her heart and body wanted to delve into Darren and find out what made him tick. He was gracious, though reserved, and clearly respected and well-liked in town. Every few minutes, someone would stop by the table to greet him. She sensed he held himself at a distance, which piqued her curiosity. Susie's comment about him being gun-shy about relationships circled through her thoughts.

When he walked her out to the car after dinner, she decided to do what she did best—be bold. She'd make it clear she was interested in one thing and one thing only. That would set her head straight and put him on notice.

Once they were in the car, Risa leaned over and slid her hand in his hair. She heard his breath catch, which sent her pulse skittering. She tried to take control and almost lost it just by touching him. His eyes met hers, that banked heat flaring to life. He was silent as he held her gaze. Her heart hammered, and she tried to remember what she meant to say.

"Let's get right to the point: I want you, and I'm pretty damn sure you want me," she finally said after gathering her scattered thoughts.

Darren lifted his hand and stroked it through her hair, his thumb caressing her neck as his hand slid down. "You'd be right about that," he replied, his voice low.

Risa could hardly think straight. Her bravado withered in the intensity of his gaze and the heat arcing between them. A tiny voice kept whispering in her mind that perhaps she was underestimating this. She ignored it and dragged her mind to her objective —keeping this light and making sure Darren understood that. "Take me to your place. Now."

He held her gaze for a long moment. Her heart pounded so hard she was afraid he could hear it. Wet heat built in her center. His thumb traveled up her neck to trace her lips before he brought his to them in a searing kiss.

There were kisses and then there were *kisses*. This was a kiss that stole her breath, dissolved all capacity for thought and wove her in its spell. His tongue followed his thumb in a soft trace around her mouth before diving into hers. He kissed her as if she was the center of the universe. Strokes, nips, licks, a tug on her bottom lip, and a fierce passion that rendered her speechless. When his mouth moved away from hers, her lips felt abandoned. She opened her eyes to find his mere inches away.

"Okay," he said softly.

She tried to remember what she'd last said and couldn't. Dazed, she stared at him blankly.

"Okay, I'll take you to my place," he clarified, a glint of a smile sneaking into his eyes.

CHAPTER 5

$\mathcal{D}$arren's brain had lost all capacity for reason the moment Risa slid her hand in his hair. He was torn between wanting her with every fiber of his being and trying to talk his body down. He liked Risa...*really* liked her. He thought he was half-crazy to consider it, but when he'd asked her to dinner, a teeny-tiny corner of his mind wondered if maybe he was ready to give the idea of a relationship a passing chance. The last time he'd been involved with a woman in any way other than casual had been before the accident. He'd been dating a perfectly nice and lovely woman named Jill. They'd only been dating a few months, but he'd thought perhaps it might go somewhere. Life had felt normal. After the accident, he couldn't seem to function normally with her. He was afraid to have her sleep with him for fear she'd witness his nightmares. He couldn't focus on much of anything because he was constantly overtired from lack of sleep. Their breakup wasn't a disaster. She'd wisely and graciously bowed out. He'd stuck to casual encounters ever since.

Until the nightmares and insomnia he experienced after his accident occurred, he'd had no clue how much lack of sleep could destroy a person. It was as if he was living underwater all the time, barely breaking the surface to get air. He'd gotten somewhat of a handle on his sleep since then with the help of his doctor here in Diamond Creek. Dr. Hanson had bluntly informed him sleep could make or break his waking life. She'd steered him away from medication despite his requests, explaining it would be better if they could find a way to help him sleep naturally. She had worked with him to structure his schedule to support his sleep and helped him identify a few supplements to help on nights when sleep eluded him. It wasn't ideal, and he still had nightmares occasionally, but he slept most nights.

Darren came to a stop at the light where he would turn to take Risa to his house. She was about to learn that the driveway he'd impulsively pulled into the other day to kiss her senseless led to his house. His brain said one thing, and his body another. He tried to talk himself down by telling himself Risa's brother was a friend. Problem was, it was more of a passing acquaintance. Trey was a great guy, but Darren would barely know him if it weren't for their connection through Jared Winters and everything that happened with Emma's ex.

His body had completely hijacked his brain as evidenced by the fact that while he was telling himself to tell her he would drop her off at her brother's house, his hands turned the steering wheel into his driveway. Once he was headed down that road, literally and figuratively, he shifted gears. *She's made it clear this is physical for her. That's all it has to be for both of you. Just enjoy it. You're not ready for anything else, but don't be stupid and pass up the chance to be with a woman this amazing.*

He came to a stop in front of his house and glanced at Risa. She was looking out the window. Her profile was arresting...and he couldn't believe he'd thought that word. Her face was sculpted, her cheekbones stood out, her chin was strong, and her lips full and sensual. Her dark hair was straight and fell in soft layers into a bob that framed her face. She turned to him, and Darren couldn't think. All he wanted was...*her.*

Moments later, they walked into his house and he watched her look around. It was close to impossible to live in Diamond Creek without a view, and his home was no exception. He was on the lower portion of the foothills surrounding Diamond Creek. His home was a small, ranch-style log home—so quintessentially Alaskan that it verged on corny. But the house was in amazing condition, and he bought it at a good price. He was nothing if not practical. The living room area had windows floor to ceiling all the way across and stylish log beams angling across the cathedral ceiling. The kitchen was on the far side from the front door through a wide entrance. A hallway on the opposite side led to three bedrooms. The view from the living room opened onto a field scattered with blue spruce and cottonwood trees with the bay and mountains beyond.

Risa walked to the windows, her eyes scanning the view. Darren set his keys on a table by the door. Before he took another step, Risa was at his side. His body rose to attention. She didn't hesitate, sliding one hand up his chest and the other around his neck, her fingers teasing into his hair. Her touch sent a current buzzing through him. In that moment, he decided he'd give her what she said she wanted.

He brought his hands to cup her face and kissed her...fiercely. He let any attempt at thought go and let instinct rule him. Risa didn't hold back, allowing her mouth to open to his and meeting him stroke for stroke. He turned her, pressing her back against the door and slid a hand down her cheek, coasting across the pulse beating rapidly in her throat, and caressing down her side, savoring the soft curve of her breast, the dip of her waist and the lush roundness of her hip. She gasped into his mouth, and he pulled back for a moment. Her eyes were inky with passion, her lips full. Their breath rose and fell in unison. Holding his gaze, confusion and uncertainty flashed in her eyes.

Though he could barely think, he gathered what little thought he had and stepped back. Risa was an unholy temptation—a woman demanding she wanted him, beautiful, bold, and so damn sexy, it nearly brought him to his knees. But there was a trace of something—he didn't know what—telling him he shouldn't dive in this fast. Her hand slipped out of his hair. "I think..." He had to pause to clear his throat, his voice raspy. "I think we need to slow down."

"No!" she replied, too sharply. Her eyes didn't match the word though. They were guarded behind the heat.

His body protested, but he forced himself to take another step back, his hand sliding off of her hip. She leaned her head against the door, her breath audible in the quiet. His own breath was just barely starting to slow down, not to mention his heart rate. His cock throbbed. He called on every ounce of restraint he had when her tongue darted out to moisten her swollen lips.

Risa met his eyes again, a rueful smile quirking her lips. "So we're slowing down then," she said, a question in her tone.

Darren took a deep breath, marshaling his thoughts and realizing he barely knew her. All he knew was the façade she tried to create—the confident woman who wanted a tumble in bed—didn't jibe with how she felt in his arms. She was anything but superficial. Her passion ran deep, and he sensed she felt things deeply. He hadn't avoided relationships the last few years because he was a jerk who wanted nothing but sex. He just hadn't quite figured out how to manage the gut-churning fear he experienced whenever he considered what it could mean to let anyone into his life and heart. It didn't seem possible that a woman like Risa could witness him in those dark, weak moments when he was felled by a nightmare and see him as anything but broken. And he couldn't stand that. It took so much to pull himself together and live a mostly normal life. He didn't think he had what it took to allow someone to see the whole of him. And yet, he couldn't seem to hold back the tide of hope for what could be with Risa.

Against reason, he stepped into the possibility of breaking the rules he'd set for himself. Though she may say otherwise, he didn't believe Risa wanted something shallow and superficial. "Yeah, we're slowing down," he replied softly. "Come here." He reached for her hand and tugged her gently away from the door. She followed, her eyes bemused.

He walked to the couch and sat down. Risa sat beside him, immediately propping her feet on a wide, cushioned ottoman. She glanced around the room before turning to him. "Lovely view outside, of course. You could use some color in here," she said with a grin.

Darren looked around the room and chuckled. To say the space lacked a feminine touch was an understatement. The walls had a few black and white photographs on them from his younger sister Hallie, a budding photographer. She'd insisted on hanging them the last time she visited. She'd also brought him the plant that sat atop one of the beams above, a philodendron draped around the beam, its green leaves a spark of color in the room. His couch was incredibly comfortable, but basic brown. Decorating was not his strong suit.

He met Risa's eyes and shrugged. "You're right. What can I say? My little sister has tried to help out a little, but she doesn't get down here too much. She's always on some kind of adventure. The adventure of the moment is a year in Greece with her boyfriend, the latest love of her life."

Risa grinned and looked around. "Well, the photos are nice, but it's..." she paused and drummed her fingers on the armrest. "...rather basic. Perhaps I could help you out a little."

The idea warmed him. He was floating in uncharted territory with Risa. He wanted her with an intensity that threw him. He sensed the same depth of attraction from her. And yet...when he'd looked into her eyes a few minutes ago, something underneath gave him pause. It was as if she was trying to convince herself of something. That glimmer of uncertainty, oddly enough, gave him the courage to step beyond his comfort zone. It wasn't that he wanted her to feel uncertain, more that he didn't feel so alone in his state of self-doubt.

He took a breath. "So, uh, about…"

She cut him off with a wave of her hand. "No need to explain. I can take a hint."

He felt her shutting him out, that warmth and passion being battened down behind walls. "I think you misunderstand why I stopped. I wasn't trying to give you a hint. I want you…*a lot.* I, uh…" He paused, running a hand through his hair. He fought with his own thoughts. He didn't know what he was saying or doing, but he needed to somehow get her to understand she mattered. "I suppose I don't know you very well…"

"Not really," she said with a wry smile.

Her smile lightened the moment. "But I'd like a chance to get to know you. I don't want to start this off on shallow footing. That's why I stopped."

Risa's smile faded. She stared at him, her eyes arcing with confusion and uncertainty again. She looked away, staring out toward the mountains. It was getting late. The sun had fallen behind the mountains. Streaks of violet, pink and gold laced through the darkening clouds. A raven called in the distance.

She turned back, her dark eyes serious. "Okay." She slipped her feet off the ottoman and turned to him. "One thing," she said softly. She leaned forward, her lips centimeters away from his. "I still want you." She closed the tiny space left between them, her lips coming against his for the barest second before she pulled back, her hand trailing down his cheek as she did.

CHAPTER 6

*R*isa walked into her office at the gallery and clicked on her computer. Sales had been strong all summer, and last week had held steady despite her unexpected absence. After a quick check of her email, she pushed away from her desk and headed out front. She did her usual walkthrough of the gallery before they opened. She straightened displays and paused to admire a new collection from a local pottery artist. She loved this place, Midnight Sun Arts. She'd met one of the owners at a painting group, the same group where she'd gotten to know Gretchen, the friend no-more who'd been Brad's side dish. The owners of Midnight Sun Arts, Ethan Westen and Jack Smith, were a longtime committed couple and hugely supportive of the arts community in Alaska. Ethan had offered Risa the job at the gallery when he heard she was looking for work. She loved working for them.

"Hey darling," Ethan said, coming to her side where she stood admiring a landscape painting. He slipped his arm around her shoulders and kissed her cheek.

Ethan was in his fifties though he easily fooled most into thinking he was still in his forties. He had black hair flecked with silver and dressed impeccably. He spent the next few minutes updating her on the latest rotation of art coming into the gallery and groused about Jack's persistent obsession with blown glass. "Something always breaks! We have to be so careful. It makes me tired. Jack refuses to capitulate, so we're stuck," Ethan said with a shake of his head.

Jack and Ethan were remarkably alike in looks and demeanor. Their primary differences seemed to be in their preferred forms of art. Ethan would have the entire gallery filled with paintings, while Jack leaned toward sculpture in various mediums from glass to metal to wood, and high-end pottery.

Ethan looped his arm through hers and began walking them toward the back office. "So how was Diamond Creek? Aside from the horrible accident, that is."

She'd called Ethan and Jack to let them know about her accident and slightly delayed return while she sorted out her car situation.

"Oh, I had a good visit. It's always good to see Trey and Emma. Stu is my sweetie, and Janet looks great." Risa paused as she pondered that all she'd been able to think about on her drive home was Darren. Even now, thinking about him flushed her.

Ethan pushed the door open to her office, closing it behind them once Risa walked in and sat in one of the chairs at a small round table near her desk. He sat opposite her and eyed her speculatively. "What are you thinking about? Or better yet, who? You're holding something back. Spill it," he said authoritatively.

She tried to dissuade him. "Ethan, it's nothing!" Her face heated even more.

He lifted a brow. "Risa, you're not much of a blusher. If you're blushing, there's a reason. If you don't tell me, I'll sic Jack on you when he gets here later."

She sighed and looked away, finally turning back to meet his warm blue gaze. "I might have met someone."

"You either met someone or you didn't. That's a factual matter."

"Okay, okay. I met someone. He's the sexiest man I've laid eyes on in years. I tried to persuade him to take a spin between the sheets, but he turned me down." As usual with Ethan, she told him everything. He and Jack were dear friends to her, but Ethan was the one she often spilled her secrets to. She'd known him longer and spent more time with him. He'd been one of her best supports after she found out about Brad and Gretchen, publicly cutting both of them every chance he got since then. In the art world of Anchorage, Ethan's social currency was quite valuable. Though satisfying to witness, it didn't heal the embarrassment Risa felt at being so stupid to fall for Brad and think things might be going somewhere.

Ethan slanted his eyes in her direction. "He turned you down flat, or something else?"

If possible, Risa flushed straight through—head to toe. Thinking back to her failed attempt at seduction and the heated kisses that led up to it was arousing and mortifying at once. She'd been internally wrestling with how to react since then. Part of her was crushed. She'd tried to be bold and failed spectacularly. And yet, part of her considered that what had occurred was anything but a failure. Darren may have turned her down in the moment, but he'd been clear it was because he liked her. Having a man as delectable as him who seemed so damn nice and generally good actually say he didn't want to rush things was an entirely new experience for her. One she couldn't quite believe. Hence, the back and forth in her brain.

Ethan cleared his throat, prompting Risa to realize she'd mentally wandered off again. Still blushing, she met his eyes. "Something else."

Ethan rolled his eyes. "You need to be a little more specific here. Is he available or not? Let's start there."

Risa giggled. "He's available. I think he's interested." She sighed. "I came on a little too strong, maybe. He put a stop to it and said he wanted a chance to get to know me."

"Well then, I like him," Ethan replied firmly. He'd pointed out to Risa many times that he thought she avoided intimacy by making it seem like all she wanted was casual sex. Though she couldn't admit it out loud, she knew he was onto something. "What's his name and how did you meet?"

"Darren. He was the first cop on the scene at my accident. And let me tell you, he looks amazing in a uniform," she offered with a grin.

Ethan chuckled. He looked across the small table at her, his eyes sobering. "Looks are nice, sometimes more than nice, but I think you've had your fill of superficial. Obviously I know next to nothing about Darren, but any man who has enough restraint to turn you down and tell you he wants to get to know you gets major points from me. You may not be my type, but trust me when I say that it would be hard for most men to turn you down."

Risa rolled her eyes. "Need I point out that you're not interested in any women ever? You've been with the love of your life for almost thirty years, and his name is Jack."

Ethan threw his head back as he laughed. "Just because the fairer sex is not my cup of tea doesn't mean I don't have a good idea of what attracts men who are interested in women. I didn't start this conversation to debate the degree of your beauty, dear. I merely wanted to point out that men are basic creatures. If this Darren managed to resist you *and* said he wanted a chance to get to know you, it's a testament to his character."

Risa suddenly wanted to cry. Because she thought Ethan was probably right, Darren seemed like a pretty good guy. It terrified her that her poor judgment might be working against her...again. But then, if he was as good as he seemed, she didn't know if she deserved someone like him. She was too flighty and had a solid track record of poor judgment when it came to men.

"Risa," Ethan said softly.

She glanced over at him, his warm blue eyes making her tears spill over.

He leaned toward the desk, grabbed the box of tissues on the corner and passed them to her. She wiped her eyes and blew her nose. "I don't know what's wrong with me."

"You have issues with intimacy, an affliction shared by many. You also happen to be the only artistic temperament in your family and have the misfortune of being a woman in a man's world. In short, you're playing with a mismatched deck in this game. Ever since I've known you darling, you've wanted to find a way to be what you think your family wants. I've met them, and they could care less. Trying to walk the straight and narrow was never going to work for you. Trey, who you look up to so much, adores you just as you are. And so you've joined the hordes of women who've dated losers. I'm a man, so I know this well. Most men are asses—I mean, my goodness, men rule the world. Literally. We think we're entitled to everything. That's where being gay is helpful—the world didn't cut me slack across the board like straight men, so I was forced to develop a minimal amount of self-reflection. Anyway, my long-winded point is this: stop giving yourself such a hard time. Maybe Darren won't be the love of your life, but he's off to a good start. So far, he's treating you with respect, and that's something you haven't had enough of as far as I'm concerned. It will do you some good to have a man woo you."

Ethan offered her a grin and blew her a kiss. His eyes glinted with mischief. "Maybe you'll have some good sex for once." His words managed to break the hamster wheel of negative chatter in her mind, so she could smile and mean it.

Risa eyed him for a long moment and tilted her head, pondering how to bring up her idea of moving to Diamond Creek. "Have you and Jack ever thought about opening a gallery in Diamond Creek?"

Ethan slapped his hand on the table and burst out laughing.

"Um, I'm not so sure what was funny about that," Risa said, starting to laugh herself simply because Ethan couldn't stop.

Still laughing, he slipped his phone out of his pocket. He finally stopped laughing and held a finger up as he tapped the screen on his phone and set it between them on the table. She saw Jack's name flash on the screen. Ethan tapped the speaker icon and waited. Jack answered.

"Hi Jack. You're on speaker," Ethan said.

"Okay, what's up?"

"You owe me dinner."

"You must be with Risa. Hi darling," Jack said.

"Hey Jack. Could one of you explain what you're talking about?" she asked.

"How about you explain, Ethan?"

Ethan grinned at her. "We had a bet on how long it would take you to ask if we'd like to open a gallery in Diamond Creek. We actually planned to do so soon, but it's taking you so damn long, we were afraid we'd have to bring in someone new to run it. I bet that you'd ask about it before the holidays this year. Jack was less decisive and tried to hedge his bets and say before next summer. I win." Ethan leaned back and crossed his arms.

Jack chuckled. "So Risa, now we can officially ask if you'd be willing to help us get it up and running."

Risa's heart leapt. She couldn't believe she hadn't asked sooner. She loved her job and considered Ethan and Jack as close as family. Her dream job was being handed to her on a platter in the place she wanted to be. "Yes! Just say when and I'll make it happen."

Ethan and Jack delved into their already well-developed plan leaving Risa to marvel they'd managed to keep this from her all this time. Not much later, they ended the call with plans for dinner with her to discuss further. Ethan stood to leave her office and paused by the door.

"Whatever you do, promise me you'll give Darren a chance to get to know you."

Risa looked up, realizing yet again how well Ethan knew her. Her best defense was offense. When that failed, she tended to withdraw. Ethan was trying to head her off at the pass. She looked at him for a long moment. "It's not like you won't make sure I do," she said with a soft grin.

CHAPTER 7

*D*arren drove down the street searching out the gallery where Risa worked. He was in Anchorage visiting his parents for the weekend. Though if he was being honest, visiting his parents was a convenient excuse to tell Risa he happened to be in town for the weekend. They'd texted back and forth a few times in the week since she'd been in Diamond Creek. He couldn't stop thinking about her —her flashing dark eyes and full lips, the brief feel of her curves against his body.

He almost missed the sign for Midnight Sun Arts. He hit the brakes and turned into the parking lot. Striding into the gallery, he found himself looking at Risa's absolutely delectable bottom as she stood on a stepladder and leaned over to adjust the corner of a painting. A man dressed in a navy suit with silvered black hair stood to the side of the ladder, casually holding it.

"How does that look?" Risa asked.

"Perfect, dear. Climb down now," the man said,

reaching a hand to steady her hip as she stepped down.

Darren experienced a flash of jealousy when the man touched Risa with familiarity. Risa wore a bright blue skirt made out of a soft fabric that clung to her curves and flared just below her knees. When she stepped off the ladder, she wobbled on the heels she wore. The man at her side grasped her arm. "Easy does it."

Risa said something Darren couldn't hear and straightened her shoulders. She took a step back, appearing to view the painting she'd hung. He decided he might as well make his presence known.

"Hey Risa," he said.

She turned quickly, her dark eyes widening at the sight of him. "Oh! Is it me or are you early?" she asked, her cheeks flushing.

The man at her side turned. Darren suddenly felt like he was being appraised. The man's sharp blue eyes blatantly assessed him. When the eyes made it back to his face, the man winked, one corner of his mouth lifting with a sly smile.

Darren cleared his throat. "Didn't you say five?" he asked, glancing at an elaborate clock on the wall made of what appeared to be hammered bronze and shaped like the sun with wild waves in the rays.

Risa followed his eyes to the clock. "I didn't even realize what time it was. I did say five," she replied with a polite smile. She glanced to the man at her side.

"This is Ethan," she said and gestured from him to Darren. "Ethan, this is Darren."

Ethan smiled widely and stepped forward, quickly shaking Darren's hand. "So nice to meet you. Risa's told me all about you," he said, his tone weighted though Darren had no idea how to interpret it.

Darren returned the handshake. "Nice to meet you too. I'd say Risa's told me all about you, but I only met her recently."

Ethan nodded, his eyes impish. "Of course. Risa's a dear friend of mine. She mentioned you were the first cop to respond when she had her accident in Diamond Creek. What a great way to meet! You got to save the day and all that. Did she mention we've asked her to help us start another gallery in Diamond Creek? Jack and I know the art world very well here in Anchorage, but I can't say I know what would sell best in Diamond Creek. Since you live there, what do you think we should focus on, paintings or sculpture?"

Risa shook her head. "Ethan, don't put him on the spot right away. He just walked through the door!"

Darren grinned and shrugged. "It's okay. I'm not going to pretend I'm an art expert, but offhand, I'd suggest both. You'll get most of your business from tourists in the summer, so you want to have options."

Ethan grinned and looked to Risa. "He doesn't mind, and he can think on his feet. That's a good thing." Ethan turned back to Darren. "It's very nice to meet you, but I have a few things to take care of. I hope to see you again soon." He winked and turned away, walking briskly to the back of the gallery.

Darren looked over at Risa who stood with her hand resting on one of the steps of the ladder. Atop the skirt that made him itch to run his hands over the soft curve of her hips, she wore a fitted cream-colored blouse, her breasts straining against the buttons.

Darren reminded himself it was his own fault he'd yet to feel those glorious breasts in his hands.

"So does Ethan own the gallery?" he asked.

Risa nodded quickly. "Along with his partner, Jack. They're amazing to work for."

She paused, looking at him uncertainly. Darren forced himself to focus. "So, uh, any preferences on where we go for dinner?"

Risa pursed her lips. "What kind of food do you like?"

"Anything."

Risa tilted her head. "Okay then, there's a great Thai place. Do you mind driving? I still haven't gotten a new car. Ethan and Jack have been taxiing me to and from work."

"Not at all. Are you ready?"

"Let me get my purse."

Darren watched Risa walk to the back of the gallery and took a moment to look around while he waited. The gallery was jam-packed with art. The walls were lined with paintings, photographs and more, while displays of various sculptures and jewelry were scattered throughout the space. Ethan came around one of the displays and stopped at Darren's side. Yet again, Darren felt as if he was under a microscope—albeit a very friendly, appreciative microscope, not that it made him feel any less self-conscious.

"So you're taking Risa out to dinner," Ethan said.

Darren nodded, wondering what was on Ethan's mind.

Ethan looked thoughtful and took a step closer, lowering his voice. "From what I see, you like Risa. I barely know you, but I have a good feeling about you.

Take my advice, she has a heart of gold, so treat her how she needs to be treated."

Darren was taken off guard, to say the least. He eyed Ethan carefully while Ethan smiled back at him. "And how would that be?"

"Let me say this, Risa is more accustomed to men who take her for granted. She's cynical as a result. If you want a chance with her, don't take her for granted."

Darren nodded slowly. "Of course. I wasn't planning to," he replied, bemused by Ethan's protectiveness and curious as to what prompted him to say anything to Darren.

The click of heels could be heard coming in their direction. Ethan took a step back and smiled benignly when Risa came into view. She glanced between them.

"Ethan, what are you up to?"

Ethan didn't even bother to pretend otherwise. "Making sure Darren knows how well you should be treated. What are friends for?" He winked at Darren and turned to walk off.

* * *

DARREN SAT across from Risa and contemplated whether the fact that he'd spent most of dinner trying to keep his lust under control would qualify as not taking her for granted. They were waiting for the check, and Darren tried to keep his eyes off of the soft skin in the shadowed place where her blouse buttoned. Dinner had been plain fun. She clearly ate at the restaurant frequently as she was on a first-name basis with everyone from the hostess to the chef who came out to greet her. Risa was an amusing companion with a dry sense of humor. She'd given him a sketch of her family history and entertained him with stories of her travels when she was younger. She clearly loved talking about art and enjoyed her work.

As they walked out, his hand naturally landed in the small of her back. He had to curb the urge to slide it down over the curve of her bottom. He managed, but barely. A short drive later, following Risa's directions, he pulled up at her apartment.

"You're coming in," she announced when he put his car in park.

"I am?"

She nodded firmly, her hair swinging softly. "Come on." She opened the door and got out, not looking back.

Darren followed her into her apartment. Her apartment was located in the upper portion of an office building in downtown Anchorage. The top three floors comprised residential apartments. Her flare for color was evident in her apartment with bright rugs and artwork through the living room and kitchen area. An easel stood in the corner of the living room. Risa kicked her shoes off and gestured for him to sit on the sofa—a plush, inviting sofa with deep cushions and throw pillows.

She walked to the kitchen. "Wine or beer?" she called out.

"Beer," he replied.

She handed him a beer and said she'd be right back.

Darren waited and wondered how to get his body under control. When he'd stopped her last week in

Diamond Creek, he'd meant what he said. He wanted a chance to get to know her. But several hours in her company was practically torture. His problem was three-fold: he wanted her badly, he liked her...a lot, and he simultaneously didn't want to treat her like a fling, while having no idea if he was ready for a relationship.

Risa returned to the living room. She settled on the couch beside him, kicked her shoes off and took a sip of wine before setting it on the coffee table.

"So what did Ethan say to you?" she asked, her eyes clear and direct.

Darren was momentarily thrown, but he eyed her carefully. He sensed it would be best to be as blunt with her as she seemed to be in general. "He told me to treat you the way you deserve to be treated."

Risa threw her head back with a laugh. "I should have known he'd say something like that." She shook her head and glanced at him again. "He's a tiny bit overprotective."

"I don't mind. It's good to have friends like him."

Risa's eyes darkened as she looked at him. Her tongue darted out to lick her lips. The desire that had been buzzing through his veins all evening notched higher.

"So have you gotten to know me yet?" she asked.

Darren began to nod before he realized where she might go with that.

"Good. Then that means you won't stop me again," she said.

Before he could form another thought, she shifted and straddled him. Her skirt rode up around her hips while his hands reflexively coasted up her thighs before he could stop himself. He'd been on the edge of desire for hours now. At the feel of her soft curves against him, his cock instantly hardened. She shifted her hips against him with a sly smile. She stroked a hand through his hair, her eyes on his, almost daring him to tell her to stop. For the life of him, he couldn't even speak though he tried to form the words. Bold as she was, her pulse fluttered in her neck when he lifted a hand and stroked a finger down her cheek. Her breath hitched, her lips falling open slightly. He was lost. With a muttered imprecation, he slid a palm up her back swiftly, lacing his fingers into the soft fall of her hair and tugging her lips to his.

CHAPTER 8

Risa had decided on the drive home that she wouldn't let Darren turn her away tonight. She wanted him so badly she was almost dizzy with it. He was an intoxicating combination of masculine with that alpha edge she loved softened by a gracious warmth. He'd been so endearing in his brief interaction with Ethan. It was clear he didn't know what to make of Ethan's blatant perusal of him, yet he hadn't been bothered by it and said it was good to have overprotective friends like him.

Once she'd clambered onto his lap and felt his cock harden against her, dizzy became demanding. When his warm palm slid up her back, strong and sure, and his hand laced in her hair and tugged her mouth to his, she was lost. Her mouth fell open, allowing his tongue to delve deeply. As she already knew, his kisses were like no other. His tongue stroked and teased, he nipped and nibbled. He tore his mouth away from hers, his lips burning a path down her neck, shivers chasing in its wake. His fingers loosened in her hair, sliding around to toy along the edge of her ear, tracing an electric path down along her collarbone into the vee where her blouse came together.

He lifted his head, his eyes meeting hers, dark and intent. She shifted restlessly against him. Her skirt had ridden up around her hips when she straddled him, and she could feel his hard shaft through the thin silk of her panties. She bit back a moan as sharp spikes of pleasure arced through her.

Moving with deliberation, his eyes holding hers, he hooked his finger in the edge of her blouse, tugging the top button open. His eyelids fell as he leaned forward and dropped a kiss. The next few moments brought her to a fevered peak as he proceeded to undo her blouse one button at a time, dusting kisses along the path of exposed skin. By the time her blouse fell open completely, she was toeing the edge of desperation. Her plan to boldly seduce him was lost in the web he wove around her.

His hands cupped her breasts, heavy and aching for his touch, through the silk of her bra. Suddenly he shifted, she felt the clasp of her bra come loose and cool air hit her skin. Her nipples, already taut, tightened at the contrast. She dragged her eyes open at the moment his mouth closed over one of her nipples. Pleasure streaked through her as she arched against him. He alternated between her breasts with suction, soft bites and licks driving her near to madness. He drew languid circles in the moisture when he pulled back, softly rolling a nipple between his thumb and forefinger.

Risa tumbled into sensation—frantic and dreamy at once. She tugged at Darren's shirt, shoving it roughly over his head. His chest was all she expected —hard planes, lean muscle, burnished gold skin—and sheer heaven to run her hands over. His breath came out in a gasp when she dragged her hands down, her nails lightly scoring his skin, coming to a stop when she reached the heat of his hard shaft and caressed it through the denim. A tiny corner of her mind was alarmed at how out of control she was, but she was helpless to rein herself in. Need spiraled through her, heat bursting in sparks behind every place he touched. Moisture built inside.

Time passed in a blur. Clothes were torn off and tossed on the floor. Risa found herself standing in front of Darren, his hands curled around her hips. She looked down into his molten chocolate gaze and almost had to look away at the bare want in the depths. He held her eyes as he slowly slid a palm down, angling across her hips through the dark curls at the apex of her thighs and into her wet folds. His thumb barely grazed across the nub of her desire, the soft touch eliciting a whimper. His other palm angled down and applied subtle pressure to open her legs. Vulnerability arced through her.

"Darren..."

His name came out in a rasp.

His brown eyes held hers.

"What are you doing?"

"Don't be afraid."

It was his eyes, not his words, that eased her fear— fear of being too exposed, too out of control.

"This...is what I'm doing."

His eyes broke away from her as he leaned forward and brought his mouth against her. She was lost. His tongue explored her folds with slow, unerring precision. Searing heart suffused her as he coaxed her closer and closer to a peak. His tongue dipped into her channel, his fingers following, establishing a steady rhythm. Fevered want pulsed through her until she flew apart, her climax ripping through her with such force that her knees buckled.

Darren's strong arms caught her as she fell against him. He swung her in his arms, easily lifting her. Still stunned from the single most powerful orgasm she'd ever experienced, her eyes met his, colliding with his intense gaze. She sensed he was barely holding himself together.

"Bed?" he asked, his voice gruff.

She weakly gestured to the short hallway. He maneuvered down the hall, turning into the door to her room when she nudged him with her shoulder. She'd left a lamp on earlier. The room was cast in soft light. He laid her carefully on the bed. For a moment, she got to take in the sight of him. She'd known he was built the day she saw him walk to her through the trees while she waited in her wrecked car. But she couldn't have imagined how glorious he would be naked. His skin was a burnished gold, every inch of him was lean muscle. He must have grabbed a condom out of his jeans before he carried her down the hall because he tore a packet open and rolled the condom on swiftly.

Darren paused to look at her, his eyes dark as they coasted over her body. She'd never felt so desired in her life—the intensity of his gaze set her pulse fluttering and moisture building again. Despite just having a mind-blowing orgasm moments ago, all she wanted was the feel of him inside of her. He moved fluidly, suddenly beside her on the bed, his heat and hardness surrounding her. His palm caressed from her shoulder, down along the curve of her breast to her hip—the rough skin skittering sparks in its wake.

Her breath caught and his eyes met hers. Without breaking his gaze, he slowly shifted his weight onto her, bracketing her face with his elbows. Her knees fell apart, and she almost came at the feel of his cock resting at her entrance. She shifted restlessly under him. He barely shifted his hips, the tip of his shaft teasing her. He did this repeatedly until she was thrashing under him, his name coming in gasps. He suddenly drove deep. He was big, stretching her, the sensation of fullness so deep and satisfying she groaned in relief.

Long strokes began, his pace steady and measured. Her desperation built as she danced along the delicious edge of another climax. When she came, it whipped through her. He finally let go of his relentless pace and surged wildly one last time, the pulses of his orgasm rippling through her.

Darren fell against her, shifting his weight to the side. Their breath echoed in the quiet room. Risa laid still, reverberations of pleasure pinging through her body. He eventually moved, sliding out of her. He got up briefly, returning to her side after stepping into the bathroom adjacent to her bedroom. Relaxed and sated, she watched him walk back to the bed, savoring the view. He met her eyes when he reached the bed, arching a brow and lifting the edge of the covers.

She wiggled out of the way while he swiftly tugged her quilt over them. He rolled against her, curling around her. She had a passing thought that she couldn't believe she felt so cherished before she fell into a deep sleep.

* * *

DARREN WOKE the next morning to the sound of the shower. He stretched and threw the covers off his body. He wondered whether it would be okay to join Risa in the shower because that was most definitely what he wanted to do. Which startled him. The depth of his comfort level with her was...like nothing he'd ever experienced. As such, it gave him pause. As he hesitated at the open door to the bathroom, he was saved from his thoughts when the water stopped running—prompting instant disappointment for him. The thought of running his hands over her luscious curves with water running all over them, well that was just delicious.

Risa stepped out of the shower and quickly wrapped a towel around her. She didn't appear to have noticed he stood by the door until he took a step. Her eyes flew up.

"Morning," he said gruffly.

She grabbed another towel and briskly rubbed her wet hair. "Good morning."

He wasn't quite sure how to read her, but she was reserved, so he elected to keep it light. "Mind if I hop in the shower before I go?"

She shook her head and slipped by him, gesturing to the shower.

After a quick shower on the cool side to tamp down the desire that surged the moment he'd met her eyes again, he dressed and walked down the hall to find her in the kitchen. She wore jeans that hugged her curves with a flowing blue blouse tied in the front just above her breasts. He had to force his eyes away from the delectable curves of her breasts above the top of her blouse.

She spoke quickly. "I'll be in Diamond Creek in a few days. Will I be able to see you?"

Darren wasn't sure what he'd expected from her, but her businesslike tone and guarded eyes didn't match her question. He decided to ignore her mixed signals and stepped in front of her, lifting a hand and tucking a damp strand of hair behind her ear.

"You can absolutely see me, but only if we don't pretend last night wasn't mind-blowing."

Her rich brown eyes widened, a flash of vulnerability darting through them. She lifted her chin slightly. "Okay," she replied, the word coming out with a soft sigh.

He decided that was enough. He dropped a soft kiss on her lips, resisting the urge to kiss her senseless and stepped away. "Call me," he said before turning to leave.

Just before he closed the door, he heard his name. He leaned his head around the door.

Risa's smile was like the sun coming out. "Last night was amazing."

CHAPTER 9

Risa spent the next few days in a flurry of planning with Ethan and Jack. They already had a well-formed business plan, having owned galleries in Seattle and Anchorage. She was tasked with the logistics, the most immediate issue for her to identify a location, preferably for them to buy. Ethan peppered hints about Darren in every interaction they had, leaving Jack to roll his eyes and assure Risa that they hadn't planned this gallery for the sole purpose of allowing Ethan to try to set her up with Darren.

It was a mere day before she was to leave for Diamond Creek, and Risa had been working almost non-stop since her evening with Darren. Her mind, or more accurately her body, kept reliving that night with him. Though the anticipation of seeing him again was almost unbearable, she was frantic to reel her hopes and dreams in. When she'd dubbed him sexy-cop the day he walked to her car in the trees, she'd known he was amazing to look at and the chemistry between them was so strong it threw her. Yet she hadn't been prepared for the intensity of actually being with him.

Until him, she considered herself in control with men. That was how she liked it. *Not how you liked it, how you could handle it.* Her mind just had to snidely point that out. Sad to say, control or not, she rarely came away satisfied from her encounters. Orgasms with men were comparable to mystical unicorns. It was another matter if she used one of her trusty toys. But with Darren...she'd been swept away, literally. Her plans to be bold and in control had dissolved under the force of the sheer madness he elicited.

All of this disoriented her. After her latest fail when it came to relationships, she wasn't feeling too confident about trying again. To be swept off her feet, to have her body scale heights she'd never thought possible in less than an hour, well that amped her hesitation up. And yet, she couldn't even contemplate not seeing him again. She could hardly keep him out of her thoughts and was deep into a daydream about him when she heard her name. She was in the back of the gallery, checking the end of day figures. They were near closing time.

Glancing up, she saw her former friend Gretchen walking toward her. Risa had only seen her a few times since the fiasco of finding out Gretchen had been seeing Brad on the side for most of Risa's relationship with him. What had hurt so much was that she'd confided in Gretchen about her insecurities about relationships, how she felt like the only person in her family who could never quite measure up. A feeling made worse by the fact that her family was nothing but supportive. It was just that whenever she looked at their lives and hers, well hers was kind of messy and slapped together. Her penchant for travel and not quite figuring out what to do with herself had her drifting until she'd met Ethan in her painting group and he'd offered her this job. Running the gallery made her feel competent and allowed her to immerse herself in the art she loved so much.

Gretchen strode toward her without hesitation. Risa looked her over. Gretchen was lovely, tall and slender with blue eyes and straight blonde hair that fell in a cascade to her waist. She dressed classically, usually in dress suits. Risa had often thought she seemed out of place in Alaska—too formal, too conservative. But she had an eye for art and enjoyed painting, which is how they'd become friends. Bitterness welled in Risa's chest. Gretchen's actions hurt more than Brad's. Risa had believed her to be a friend.

Gretchen came to a stop on the opposite side of the glass case that doubled as a counter. "Hi," she said simply.

Risa schooled her expression to blank and waited. Silence loomed between them. Gretchen shifted her weight from one hip to the other. She sighed elaborately.

"Risa, don't you think it's time to move on?"

"I have moved on."

"No, you haven't. We were friends long before Brad ever dated you. Why would you sacrifice our friendship over him?" Gretchen asked, her tone laced with annoyance.

Risa couldn't hold her silence any longer. "I didn't sacrifice our friendship over him. You did. I *never* would have done to you what you did to me. That's not what friends do. Next time your friend's boyfriend hits on you, you turn him down no matter how tempting it is and immediately tell your friend that her boyfriend's a loser. I do need to thank you for illuminating what an asshole Brad was, but I no longer consider you a friend."

Risa was furious and had to struggle to keep her composure though it was satisfying to call Gretchen out. She wasn't about to allow herself fall apart in front of Gretchen. She had moved on in the sense that she didn't have any lingering feelings for Brad. But the situation stung. It hurt like hell to learn she'd been such a fool. She wondered why Gretchen was coming to her now. It had been months and months. Last Risa had heard, Gretchen and Brad had moved in together. Much as she would have liked to avoid both of them, the world of art was small in Alaska and their circles bumped against each other.

"Why are you here, Gretchen?"

Gretchen's mouth tightened and subtle flush crested her cheeks. "I lost my job at Lupine Gallery. I know why you wouldn't want to help, but I thought maybe you might be willing to give me a reference," she said baldly.

Risa's mouth fell open. The sheer gall of Gretchen blew her mind. "What?"

Gretchen lifted her chin, flushing more deeply. "Look, I apologized about what happened. I get that we won't be friends again, but you know how well I know art. I need a good reference to get in some of the local galleries. You painted with me for years and worked with me on a number of local events. It's not crazy for me to ask."

Risa shook her head abruptly. Though Gretchen

had a point, she also had plenty of other people to ask. "I'm afraid you'll have to ask someone else."

Ethan came out from the door behind the counter that led to the offices and storage. Gretchen ignored him. "You're not welcome here," he said flatly, walking around the display case to her side.

Gretchen held Risa's gaze for another moment before her eyes dropped and she turned away. Ethan silently escorted her outside, quickly returning.

"What did she want?" he asked, coming to Risa's side.

Risa looked at Ethan and couldn't help but smile. His usually warm blue eyes were angry, his gaze protective. She considered how she felt after Gretchen's ridiculous request and clumsy attempt to gloss over what her actions had done to their friendship. She felt strangely okay. Her anger had dissipated in the clarity of the situation. Gretchen represented all that she didn't want to be.

"I'm fine," she said firmly.

Ethan gave her a confused look. "I'm glad you're fine, but what does that have to do with what she wanted?"

Risa burst out laughing. "You're not going to believe what she wanted. First, she wanted us to be friends again, or so she said…"

Ethan interrupted. "Oh my God! How dare she!"

Risa put her hand on his arm. "Oh, it gets better. I don't think she really wanted to be friends again. What she wanted was to ask me to be a reference for her. She lost her job at Lupine Gallery and is scrounging around for references. Don't worry, I said no. And you know, I'm glad she stopped by."

Ethan eyebrows almost flew off his forehead as he

kept shaking his head. "I cannot believe her. The nerve!" He paused and glanced sideways at her. "You're glad she stopped by?"

Risa nodded. "At first, I wasn't. But it was very... illuminating. She made me realize I have moved on, and that's a good thing."

Ethan stared at her and finally shrugged. "Okay then. I'm glad to hear it. Meanwhile, I'll do my best to make sure no one hires her."

* * *

RISA WALKED along the boardwalk that connected a run of buildings on a beach in view of Otter Cove Harbor. Ethan and Jack had given her a list of places they'd researched online. They wanted her to check them out before contacting realtors. She'd visited three locations thus far, all striking out in her estimation. This place was last on their list. Several stretches of oceanfront property in Diamond Creek were prime retail locations with clusters of buildings along boardwalks. There was a mix of arts, clothing, sporting goods and restaurants ranging from basic to high-end, all enjoying an amazing view that drew tourists from all over the world.

She paused in front of an art gallery with a For Sale sign on the building. Ethan and Jack had conferred with the owner about purchasing the business and building with the intent to gradually shape the gallery to their preferences. She stepped inside, immediately into a cluster of shoppers. A quick look around let her know the location would be ideal though the current owners certainly didn't share Ethan and Jack's taste in art. They appeared to have focused too exclusively on kitschy items, which held their own unique appeal, but could rarely bring in enough to keep a business afloat.

Risa meandered through the gallery before making her way back outside. She followed the boardwalk to the beach. Kachemak Bay spilled out in front of her, mountains rising tall across the bay, glaciers glowing that other-worldly blue in the valleys, and Mount Augustine, the volcano that sat sentry in the distance, anchoring the view. A salty breeze ruffled the water, and boats moved in and out of the harbor. An eagle sat on a piece of driftwood nearby, its gaze trained on the water. As she began walking along the edge of the water, a pair of seals surfaced, watching her curiously. She considered that if she moved here, she'd be able to walk along this beach whenever she wanted. She kept walking, collecting a few rocks as she did, pausing to place a starfish left behind by the tide back in the water.

When she returned to her car, for the first time in too long, her mind was quiet. The beach did that to her. She quickly texted Ethan and Jack to tell them this place had definite potential. They would be down for a follow up visit with the realtor in the next few days. She began to pull out of the parking lot as an approaching vehicle was turning in. She thought they were going a little too fast and jumped at the sound of squealing tires. With an abrupt thump, the car skidded against hers. Her car swayed underneath her, and she slammed on the brakes.

"Dammit! I just got this car two days ago," Risa said to no one. She'd finally decided on a used car to replace the vehicle totaled in her last visit to Diamond Creek. She put her car in park and got out.

If the driver of the other car were over the age of twenty, she'd be amazed. The driver was a young man, all arms and legs. She could hear whom she presumed to be his mother exclaiming that he hadn't been paying attention. Annoyed as Risa was, one look at the boy and she felt bad for him.

He slowly climbed out, his face bright red. "I'm sorry. I think I didn't slow down enough when I turned," he said.

The woman with him came around the car. They shared matching blonde hair and blue eyes. "I'm so sorry. Eric is still getting used to driving. He has a serious lead foot and won't slow down no matter how many times I tell him to be careful." She glanced to Eric with a shake of her head. "I'm Shannon, by the way. Let me get our insurance information." She scurried back around the car and began rummaging through the glove compartment.

Eric's face flushed an even deeper shade of red. He sagged against the car, appearing resigned to having to suffer through this event.

"Nice to meet you," Risa replied to Shannon's back. "It's okay. All he did was bump me. Don't even worry about the insurance thing right now. How about you let me get an estimate first?" Risa asked.

"Are you sure?" Shannon asked.

Risa nodded. "It'll probably be less than your deductible." She paused and glanced at her car. It wasn't even dented, just scraped. "I'm Risa, by the way."

Shannon came back around the car and brushed her hair out of her face with a sigh. "That would be great if you don't mind. He's only seventeen, so you can imagine how much the insurance will be if we have to report this."

"Oh shit," Eric said.

"Eric! Do you have to swear so much?" Shannon said, her tone sharp as she glared at him.

Risa followed his eyes to see a police cruiser headed their way. Her heart instantly lurched, wondering if it was Darren. This followed with a sigh when she realized if it were him, this was accident number two for her in the last few weeks, which only reinforced her 'bumbling through life' image. The police cruiser got close enough that she could see it was Darren. She'd texted him this morning to let him know her schedule for the day, but they hadn't confirmed anything.

Darren pulled into the parking lot through another entrance with their cars blocking this one. Risa reconsidered her ability to control herself as he approached them. He was all sexy cop. Damn if that uniform didn't just make everything about him better. She wondered whether they designed the uniforms to be so fitted. His muscled shoulders, chest and arms were accentuated by the navy shirt that hugged him like a glove. He'd been on his phone when he approached and only when he was a few feet away did he look up. As soon as he saw her, he grinned. She swooned inside and had to force herself to focus because she had to keep up appearances in front of poor Eric whose face was neon red at this point.

"Hey there, what happened here?"

Shannon began talking rapidly. "Eric took the corner too quick and scraped her car."

Risa decided an interruption might be good about now. "It's nothing. We've already sorted it out."

Darren met her gaze, his chocolate brown eyes almost melting her on the spot. She tried telepathy, but he didn't seem to be getting her message when he arched his brow. "Let me check..."

Risa stepped to his side. "There's nothing to check. Don't give Eric a ticket. He barely bumped my car. Let's call this one a pass. If it happens again, then you can give him a ticket." She had no idea why she was so determined to make sure Eric didn't get a ticket, but he looked so genuinely remorseful that she wanted to cut him a break.

Darren eyed her for a long minute and then shrugged. "Fair enough." He turned to Eric. "You ran into a nice person today. Count yourself lucky and remember that I will know if you make a habit of this. Here's the deal: no ticket for you if you promise you'll mow the lawn in front of the station for the rest of the summer. We'll pay you, and you can immediately turn the money over to your mom to go towards your car insurance."

Eric, his face still bright red, pushed away from the car. "Yes sir," he said barely above a mumble. "When should I come do the lawn?"

"How about next week? And honestly, we're headed into fall, so you're only going to have to mow for a month or so." Darren looked to Shannon. "That work for you?"

Risa was awash in silly joy for a moment at Darren's easygoing response. This was instantly followed with the realization that she didn't know if she could measure up to him. But damn if she didn't just *like* him. On top of everything, he kept showing her he was as good as he seemed on the surface. Flustered, she tried to keep from grinning like an idiot and forced herself to look away from him.

Shannon beamed. "Absolutely!" She turned to Risa. "Call me when you get that estimate. You want to put my number in your phone?"

They quickly exchanged numbers before Eric and Shannon climbed back in the car to park and head into one of the sports shops.

A gust of wind blew Risa's hair wild. Darren leaned against her car, his eyes trained on her. "That was nice of you."

She shrugged, brushing her hair out of her face when another gust blew by. "He's only seventeen. If he gets a ticket, they'll be paying through the nose for years on insurance. He barely scraped my car. He looked so sad about it, I couldn't help it. Not to mention that in a town this size, you'll know if he's careless again."

Darren nodded. "He won't be. He's a good kid. That's why I went along with you," he said with a smile, his eyes darkening.

"Do you usually get kids to mow the lawn at the station?" she asked with a grin.

Darren chuckled. "Yep. The last kid finished his duty last week, so the timing was perfect."

Quiet fell between them. Gulls called nearby. An eagle swooped to land on a piling by the corner of the parking lot, gazing right at them. Risa suddenly felt self-conscious and then thought she must have lost her mind if an eagle made her feel that way.

Darren caught her eyes and nodded toward the eagle. "It's their eyes."

She flushed, realizing he had picked up on her

feeling. "They're so, I don't know, intense. It's like they can see through you."

He grinned before his gaze sobered quickly. In a flash, a current came to life between them. Darren's eyes made her feel…alive, uncertain, desired, and so much more.

"So how did the store hunting go?" he asked, his mundane question belying the way she felt.

"Out of four, I found one good possibility." She pointed to the gallery nearby.

"Ah, that place went up for sale last month. They stay busy, but it's small stuff, so I doubt it's enough to keep them afloat."

"Exactly what I thought. We'll buy it as is and rework the inventory. Ethan and Jack will be down in a few days to meet with the realtor."

He nodded. His eyes searched her face, and heat spiraled through her. Trying to marshal her composure, she looked out over the water. The wind had picked up, churning small whitecaps across the bay. Rather than calming, her pulse raced. Just being near Darren and she was grasping for control. The feeling was alternately thrilling and terrifying. She liked to feel in control and to be left grasping at a tenuous thread of it was unsettling.

"So how long will you be here?"

His voice drew her back. Turning to look at him, she swatted away thoughts of how amazing his mouth felt against hers. "I'm here for at least a week right now. After that, I'll get busy figuring out the move."

"You're really moving here?"

She flushed and nodded. "The only thing that might have kept me in Anchorage was the fact that I love my job. With Ethan and Jack handing me the job here on a silver platter, there's no way I'd say no."

Darren nodded, his eyes inscrutable. He pushed away from her car, coming to stand right in front of her. Heat emanated from his body, or so Risa thought. It was either that or her off-the-rails imagination when it came to Darren. "So, uh, when can I see you?" he asked.

"You're seeing me right now," she said with a grin.

He rolled his eyes. "That I am, but that's not what I meant and you know it."

"How about dinner tomorrow? I have a nephew who would be very disappointed if I wasn't at dinner there tonight."

He nodded, his eyes holding hers for a long moment before he stepped back. They were in a busy area with tourists milling around on the beach and at the shops, and traffic all around. Much as Risa wanted to reach out and tug him to her for one of those incredible kisses, she knew it probably wouldn't do for the chief of police to be making out in downtown Diamond Creek. She savored the sight of him walking back to his police cruiser before climbing in her car.

CHAPTER 10

$\mathscr{D}$arren woke abruptly sitting bolt upright and then sagging back against the pillows. His heart was racing. He rarely remembered his dreams—just flashes of motion, sound, and the echoing sense that he'd lost something. He lay still in the dark as his heartbeat slowed. An owl called softly from the yard. Risa filled his thoughts, a welcome respite from his usual mental meanderings in the night. He'd almost laughed when he pulled up and realized she'd managed to get in a fender bender through no fault of her own. Her insistent kindness to Eric only increased his interest in her. *And just what the hell do you plan to do about it? You can't hide this mess if you plan to do something other than have a fling.* He kicked the covers off and headed to the shower.

Hours later, he strode across the parking lot toward the station. Cool wind blew in gusts. Though it was still technically summer, fall weather had made a few appearances with today the coolest yet. The brisk air blew the door wide when he stepped through. He headed straight for the kitchen to grab a cup of coffee, savoring the warmth. Before he managed to get to his office, his radio went off, reporting a domestic disturbance. As he turned to head back out, Sylvia came down the hall and grabbed his coffee right out of his hands.

"Hey, what...?" he asked her back as she kept walking into the kitchen.

With a shake of his head, he briefly stepped into his office and grabbed a fleece jacket hanging on the door. He hadn't bothered to pay attention to the weather before leaving his house this morning. By the time, he stepped back in the hall, Sylvia stood there with a travel mug.

"I can't let you walk out of here without this," she said with a warm smile while handing him the travel mug.

He chuckled. "What would I do without you?"

She shrugged. "You'd get by just fine, but you might miss out on coffee when it's too busy."

She followed him as he moved to the door. "The call is for a domestic disturbance right on Main Street."

Darren nodded. "Let me guess, it's the Moulton's."

Sylvia rolled her eyes. "Most likely. I'd bet you on it, but they live at the apartment complex, so could be anyone there."

He hit the door with his shoulder and pushed through, lifting his travel mug as he turned away. "Thanks for getting my coffee to go."

Within the hour, Darren climbed back in his patrol car with a sigh. As predicted, the call was from Rick and Lisa Moulton's apartment, a young couple with a penchant for late nights, heavy drinking and arguments that escalated out of control. They were so predictable, he and the other officers could practically schedule visits to their apartment every few weeks. Charlie Brooks, his usual partner who'd heard the call on his way in and headed straight there, had joined Darren at the call. Charlie had left a few minutes earlier with Rick in handcuffs and headed for a brief stay in jail. Lisa usually declined to press charges and often refused to cooperate with interviews, which tended to leave Darren with few options. This time was different since the neighbor was a witness.

Darren headed over to Misty Mountain Café, his favorite local bakery. He rarely bothered with breakfast and was downright starving. The café was crowded when he entered. He threaded through the cluster of tourists and snagged a few ham and cheese savories before making his way to the back of the line.

He felt a nudge on his shoulder and looked back to find Travis.

"As usual, I find you here," Travis said by way of greeting.

"Could say the same to you."

Travis grinned. "Well, they have the best bakery in town and damn good coffee. How's it going?'

"Started the day out with a visit to the Moulton's."

Travis shook his head. "The usual, I'm guessing."

"Only difference today was a neighbor happened to be outside when he saw Rick haul off and punch Lisa, so we actually got to arrest him."

Travis merely shook his head again. "It's sad when I think that's good news. I'm about ready for summer to wind down. It's been a busy fire season."

"I know. This has been one of the rougher years—

too dry. With all the beetle kill, dry years are a nightmare."

Travis nodded as they stepped forward in the line. He nudged Darren's shoulder again. "Hey, it's that woman we helped after her car accident the other week."

Darren followed Travis' eyes to see Risa seated at a table with Emma Holden, her sister-in-law. A glance at Risa and his pulse kicked up a notch. Her dark hair fell loosely around her face. He'd yet to see her in anything other than bright colors and today was no exception. A bright red blouse topped a pair of fitted jeans. When she laughed at something Emma said, her head went back, eliciting the memory of her neck arched back the other night. Just like that, lust surged through him. This near obsession with a woman was…unusual. He couldn't stop thinking about her.

Travis cleared his throat. Darren tore his eyes away from Risa, glancing back to Travis who arched a brow.

"What?" Darren asked.

"You were seriously staring, that's what."

Darren flushed and opened his mouth to deny it before grinning. "You caught me."

"What's her name again?"

Darren couldn't believe Risa hadn't seared herself into Travis's memory as she had his, which only reinforced the reality that he appeared to have temporarily lost control of his faculties when it came to her. "Risa, her name's Risa."

Darren stepped to the front of the line to order his coffee and pay. Travis stepped away with him. "Catch you later," Travis commented. He followed Darren's eyes to Risa. "I suggest you walk over and say hello, seeing as you can't keep your eyes off of her." Travis cuffed him on the shoulder before walking away.

Darren took a breath and reminded himself he'd follow this feeling out with Risa, and it would wear off. That's how it needed to be. He wasn't ready for more, not when he knew she'd see him as broken if she got too close. In the meantime…

"Hey there," he said stepping up to the table where Risa sat with Emma. Emma and Trey's baby daughter, Janet, was napping in a car seat tucked by Emma's chair on the floor.

Risa looked up, her rich velvety brown eyes meeting his. She looked surprised. "Oh, hi."

Emma smiled widely at him. "Darren, so good to see you." She tucked her long dark hair behind her ears. "How are you?"

"Pretty good. Just stopped by to say hi."

Emma nodded and started to say something when her phone, which sat on the table, rang loudly. "Oh sorry, I have to get this." She stood quickly, gesturing to Janet.

Risa nodded and waved her off. Quiet fell between them, the hubbub of voices around them filling the space. Risa looked up at him. He wanted to lean over and feast on those decadent lips of hers. A flush stained her cheeks. Darren realized he must have been staring again.

He cleared his throat and drew on the manners his mother had drilled into him. "How are you today?"

She rewarded him with a smile and a small shrug. "Pretty good. I was hoping to see you tonight," she said simply.

Darren's pulse, which was barely in check, rocketed again. He nodded. "No family plans tonight?"

She shook her head and took a sip of coffee. "Nope. Tell me when and where," she said, her eyes shifting away.

He followed them to see Emma heading back in their direction, pocketing her phone. "How about you meet me at my place?"

She nodded quickly just as Emma reached the table. "How did she do?" Emma asked, glancing down at her daughter.

Risa tilted her head and rolled her eyes. "Seriously Emma, you were gone for less than five minutes. She didn't even open her eyes." Risa glanced up at him. "Janet's only three months old and Emma's first baby. She worries a bit much," she said with a grin.

Emma appeared entirely unfazed. "Tease all you want," she retorted. "You just wait until it's your turn."

Darren's mind instantly started going down a road he'd barred himself from—wondering what it would be like to be the man at Risa's side when it was her turn to start a family. The desire to be that man was so visceral it shocked him. His gut churned as he shook his head to get the image out of his mind. Not a dream he could have.

* * *

RISA FLEW THROUGH HER DAY. Ethan and Jack had already scheduled to meet later today with a local realtor to view the one possible location she'd identified. Meanwhile, she spent most of her morning and early afternoon updating the inventory in their online database and visiting the town offices to get permits in place.

Late that afternoon, she walked out of the gallery

with Ethan and Jack. "Well?" she asked, turning to them.

Ethan nodded firmly. "This is perfect."

Jack tilted his head, his short silver hair glinting in the sun. "It's not exactly perfect, but it's flawed enough that we can get a good deal, which makes it perfect," he said with a sly grin.

Ethan chuckled. "Precisely."

Two pair of blue eyes looked back at her. "So how are we doing on everything else?" they asked in unison.

Risa never failed to be amused at how alike they were. They'd been together so long, they often spoke simultaneously. "All the necessary paperwork has been submitted. The town office said we'd have the license to operate by the end of this week. What did your realtor say about the timeframe? I missed that part of the conversation."

"Apparently, the sellers are moving out of state, so they're happy to hand over the reins as soon as they legally can. We've asked for a fast turnaround on the appraisal, so hopefully it will be by the end of this month. In the meantime, we're thinking we'll head back to Anchorage to keep hands on deck on the gallery there, and you can do the rounds here to scope out our competition. Let's try to get a sense of what we can offer that won't be more of the same," Jack said.

"So, how's Darren?" Ethan asked, his eyes glinting with mischief.

Risa rolled her eyes. "He's fine. I'm meeting him for dinner tonight."

Jack arched a brow. "Well, well. Here I thought Ethan was making more of this than it was."

Risa flushed but managed not to take the bait. After they left, she climbed in her car. Her plan tonight was to get back in control with Darren. Oh, she'd meant what she said—she wanted to see him tonight. *Like you've never wanted anyone before.* Her subconscious stealthily interrupted, and she batted it away. No matter how much he unbalanced her, she could get this back on firm footing. She would be able to keep it light and fun and have more of the best sex of her life all at the same time. As long as she could do that, it wouldn't matter if he ended up letting her down, or worse, ended up making her want more than she could have.

CHAPTER 11

Smoke bellowed out from under the hood of Risa's new-to-her car. She'd turned down what she thought was Darren's road too quickly to realize it wasn't when the road went from pavement to dirt and no houses came into view. Right after she'd done a twenty-point turn to head back from where she came, the temperature needle on her dashboard climbed rapidly and her engine made a loud humming sound following by a pop. She climbed out and glanced around. The sky was dark with clouds, the air heavy with the threat of rain.

"Dammit!"

A magpie flew low with a burst of chatter before landing on a spruce tree nearby. Risa kicked at a tire before flinging her door open and grabbing her purse. She knew she wasn't far from Trey's house or Darren's, but she didn't know exactly where she was. She hemmed and hawed for a moment, trying to decide if she wanted to call Darren or Trey and Emma. Calling Darren meant he'd see her yet again dealing with car problems though at least this time it wasn't an accident. The depth of her yearning to see him was so strong, she couldn't *not* call him. If she called Trey and Emma, it could derail her entire evening. Though she planned to be in complete control, she didn't want to miss out on seeing Darren. He didn't answer, so she left a message that ended with a confusing attempt to tell him where she was.

Why the hell did you leave him that message? Because he was going to see I called, so I might as well explain. You sounded like an idiot. Risa leaned against her car with a groan. She was talking to herself. That's how idiotic she was. She shoved away from the car and walked back to the front, eying the hood. The smoke had slowed down, but she didn't have it in her to open the hood and check. She prayed it wouldn't rain.

The road she'd ended up on had no houses on it and trees rising tall on both sides. A canopy of spruce interspersed with cottonwood and birch enveloped the road. Birds flitted in the trees. The air was cool, soft and earthy scented. The quiet was broken by the sound of a car. Darren stopped his patrol car in the middle of the road and got out. She soaked in the view of him. He'd changed out of his uniform and wore faded jeans that molded over his muscled legs. A cotton jersey shirt clung to his shoulders and chest— almost making her salivate at the thought of what was underneath. He strolled over to her car and grinned.

"What's so funny?" she asked, instantly annoyed at his amusement with her predicament.

His grin merely widened. "You and cars don't seem to get along too well. How did you end up here?" he asked, gesturing at the road.

She looked up and down the road. "I thought it

was your road!" She fought to keep from smiling but his grin was contagious, not to mention having him anywhere near her made her insides do a happy dance.

He walked to the hood of her car and stared at it. After a long moment, he shrugged.

"What? Can you tell what's wrong with it?"

He burst out laughing.

She stomped over to his side. "This isn't funny!"

His brown eyes met hers. She fought against the stealthy curl of desire sliding through her veins.

"Okay, okay. I don't mean to make light of it. Three out of four times I've seen you, something happens to your car, that's all."

She rolled her eyes and purposefully moved away from him, her plan to be in control already on shaky ground. For crying out loud, her car was overheated, it was about to rain, he stopped to help, and all she could think about was pushing him up against the car and kissing him. Annoyed as she was, he had a point, and she could laugh at the situation.

With a rueful grin, she shrugged. "Fair enough. I do seem to have a pattern of car issues lately. Do you think I can try starting it again?"

She looked toward the front of the car to see smoke still snaking out from under the hood.

Darren walked to where she stood beside the car, resting one hand on the roof. "Nope. I was thinking about asking you to open the hood, but I realized that was pointless, which is why I laughed. I don't know what's wrong, but I definitely know it's not a good idea to try to do anything with that much smoke coming out."

Risa's brain filled with static at Darren's nearness.

She took a step away, only to find her back up against the car.

"So does anyone live on this road?" she asked, grasping for anything to get her mind off of his chocolate eyes and those lips she knew felt amazing. Her eyes bounced away and landed on his well-developed chest. She could feel the heat from his body. Her heart pounded and heat swirled in her center.

Darren looked briefly up and down the road before his eyes landed on hers again. His mouth lifted at one corner as he shook his head. "Nope. This is an old right-of-way. Some guy planned to build down here and had it paved halfway. Not sure what happened, but he hasn't built anything yet. My road is another mile or so down the hill."

His eyes stayed on hers. Risa's brain seemed to have stopped functioning entirely—other than thoughts about what it would feel like to kiss him again and run her hands over his body. Moisture built between her legs, her breath became short, and she couldn't focus on anything beyond the heat of his eyes.

Mentally fumbling, she forced herself to try to focus. "So, uh, is there someone I can call to tow my car? Or should I…"

Her words were cut off when he put his finger on her lips.

"We can call the tow place in a minute. First I need to do this."

His voice was low and gruff. Before she could formulate a thought, much less a response, he moved swiftly, bringing his lips to hers. His tongue swept inside, instantly wiping all thought clear. Lust streaked though her. Her mouth opened to his, and their kiss went wild. Darren turned to face her, pressing her against the car. The contrasting heat from his body with the cool metal of the car against her back escalated the flurry of feeling coursing through her.

She forgot any plan to stay in control and abandoned herself into the moment. Tugging him against her, she gloried in the feel of his muscled body. Her pulse careened out of control. She slid her hands up under his shirt, just like she wanted, skating across his warm skin, over his muscles and around his back, the corded tendons delicious under her hands. He tore his lips from hers, his hand stroking into her hair. He lightly nipped her earlobe, his lips traveling down the side of her neck, shivers chasing in their wake.

She felt hot and achy, her clothes tight and constricting. She moaned in relief when he tore her blouse open, cool air hitting her skin. He stopped moving, and she opened her eyes to find his trained on her.

"Dear God, you're beautiful," he whispered.

Her breasts rose and fell with her breath. He lifted his eyes to meet hers, and she became more lost than she already was. The intensity and depth of plain desire in his gaze took her breath away. She scrambled, trying to gather her wits. But he seemed to slip in under her defenses simply by being close to her. She watched as his hand, strong and warm, came up to curl around her breast. He rolled her nipple, peaked tight under the lacy silk of her bra, between his thumb and forefinger. A whimper escaped her. His eyes flicked up. Holding her gaze, his thumb slipped under the clasp between her breasts. With a snap, her bra fell open. Pinned in place by his dark eyes, she couldn't look away as he lowered his head slowly, his eyes only breaking from her when his lips softly closed around a nipple. The touch of his mouth was electric, sending a jolt through her.

She arched against the car, rolling her hips against the heated length of his cock. His lips alternated between soft dusting kisses, gentle nips and a sharp bite on her nipple. Yearning surged through her, escalating to a frenzy. Rain began to fall; the cool drops on her skin a balm to the heat inside of her. His lips made their way back up her neck to her mouth, coming against hers. He gentled their kiss by increments. When he pulled away, his mouth mere inches from her, she only wanted him not to stop. She gulped in air and met his eyes.

Rain fell steadily. His lashes spiked with the moisture, raindrops rolled down his face. She tilted her head back, savoring the cool water as it fell against her face. Looking back at him, a frisson of awareness stole up her spine. She didn't know what this was between them, but it was beyond her experience. Touching him was like breaking the surface of water after too long underneath. She felt alive, exhilarated, relieved and shaken all at once. It wasn't mere physical attraction, and *that* made her feel exposed. On the heels of that feeling, her heart ached to turn to Darren to soothe her. That's what he did to her—stole her senses, scrambled her thoughts, and made her forget how much she needed to be in control. A shiver raced through her, the cool air chilling her, her bare skin pebbling in the rain.

His chest rose and fell against hers in a deep breath. He held her eyes steadily in the rain, reaching up to brush a drop of rain off her lashes.

He cleared his throat. "Let's get out of the rain before you get too cold," he said gruffly.

She couldn't seem to find words, so she nodded. He stepped back and hooked her bra together before efficiently buttoning her blouse. She closed her eyes, trying to stop the trembling inside and the fear crashing through her. *You can't want him this much. It's not sane. Don't be stupid and fall for someone again.*

"Risa?"

His voice broke through her thoughts. Her eyes flew open, colliding with his, which were warm and steady.

"Let's get in my car and call the tow truck from there." He tugged her gently away from her car.

She followed him through the rain, sighing when he closed the door for her. Inside, she was glittering, sparks of passion dancing through her veins. Her emotions were taut—pulled tight like a string with the depth of her want for Darren, a force she couldn't harness, tempting and terrifying beyond measure. Once he was in the car, he quickly made a call, assuring the tow truck driver they'd wait until he was there. A soft silence fell around them when he ended the call. Rain pattered on the roof while Risa wondered how it could feel so...*right* to be with him.

* * *

Darren looked across the room at Risa where she stood by the front windows looking out into the rain. Her dark hair was still damp and tousled from the rain. Her blouse clung to her generous curves. He'd planned to take her out to dinner, but she'd waved it off, commenting she was too wet to go out. So he'd scrounged through his pantry, only to have her nudge him with an elbow before taking over and rustling up a quick pasta dish with seasoned olive oil and the fresh tomatoes he only happened to have because Sylvia had brought some in from her garden for everyone at the station.

Risa stood with her hands tucked in the pockets of her fitted jeans. As with her blouse, the denim hugged her curves tightly, reminding him of how phenomenal it felt to curl his hands around her lush hips. She'd been slightly subdued since those earth-shattering moments by her car in the rain. He'd only meant to kiss her briefly, just to have a taste of her lips, before calling for the tow truck and taking her out to dinner. But the second his lips met hers, thought had fled on the heels of sensation surging and burning through him. It unsettled him because he wanted her in a way he'd never experienced. He told himself he wanted the chance to get to know her and didn't want this to be purely physical. And yet, the draw was so strong, it completely took over when he was near her. Flitting in the back of his mind when he could think at all, he scrambled to keep purchase. He hadn't spent an entire night with a woman in years...until the other night with her in Anchorage. His habit was to leave long before dawn, but he hadn't been able to bring himself to roll out of bed and leave Risa sleeping there alone. Being with her felt too damn good. He felt lucky to come out of it without waking in a cold sweat, without her looking at him with questions in her eyes —like his girlfriend at the time of the accident. She'd spent a few nights with him after the accident—each time looking at him with concern and a tinge of pity, which he could hardly stand.

But Risa...she was the first woman who tempted him to reconsider anything. He thought perhaps he would have appreciated the no-nonsense approach he sensed from her at first—that she only wanted a casual fling, no strings. Instead of having the sense to appreciate it, he wanted to see inside her heart and understand why she was so guarded. She masked her reserve with boldness. *And you're damn crazy to think like this. You can't let her matter this much. She's got her own baggage, and you've got more than enough to carry on your own. If she gets a clue of how heavy your baggage is, she'll turn tail and run. Or worse, she'll pity you.*

Darren shook his head sharply and strode to join Risa by the window. Rain fell steadily, graying the view. The mountains loomed dark in the fading light and rain. Wind whipped across the bay, roiling the water with whitecaps. He heard a soft sigh and glanced at Risa. When she turned reflexively toward him, her dark brown eyes flashed with feeling, which she immediately shuttered. He couldn't halt the wish to peel away the layers she hid behind.

"It feels like fall is almost here," she said, her words dropping like soft pebbles in the quiet room.

His eyes locked to hers, he nodded. "It is. Almost here, that is. There's not much of a fall in Alaska. But you know that. One day it's summer, the next day it's fall with winter days on the way."

He forced his eyes away and looked out the window. A raven flew by the window, calling through the rain and landing on the bough of a spruce tree. He heard Risa's breath and turned back, just in time to see her tongue dart out to moisten her lips.

Lust jolted through him. He swore and swatted

caution away. "Risa," he rasped, his voice husked with want.

Her eyes held his, vulnerability flashing through them, but she lifted her chin and held his gaze. He moved slowly, bringing his hand up to thread in the silky fall of her hair. Her breath came out in a soft exhalation as he stepped closer to her, the heat of her body a magnet for his. As he leaned forward, he slipped his hand down to cup her cheek, his thumb stroking the line of her jaw. Her eyes darkened, her chest rose and fell in a quick breath. He tried, oh how he tried, to kiss her gently. He failed...utterly and completely. The second his lips met hers, it was as if a flame twined around them. He stroked deeply into her mouth, savoring how quickly she opened to him. She pressed up against him, the feel of her breasts against his chest intoxicating. Any intent he had to draw this out, to make it slow, was lost in the maelstrom of desire that washed around and within them. He needed her like the air he breathed.

He moved swiftly, lifting her in his arms. She gasped and her eyes flew wide. In two quick strides, he lowered her to the couch and stood. Her dark hair framed her face, her lips bright red in the gray light. He reached over and switched on a lamp nearby.

He couldn't think. All he wanted was her skin bared to him. He tore his shirt off and leaned over, resting one hand on the back of the couch while he trailed the back of his other hand across her cheek, down her neck where her pulse fluttered, and into the vee of her blouse. He methodically unbuttoned her blouse and flicked her bra open, groaning when her breasts spilled free. He forced himself to hold back because he wanted to see all of her. No words passed between them—only the give and take of the living, breathing force shimmering around them. Her nails trailed across his chest, her palm cupped his cock—so hot and hard—through the denim of his jeans. Her jeans were torn off, and his were kicked off. She sat before him on the couch, nothing but a scrap of bright blue lace covering what he wanted most. He hooked his thumb under the edge and dragged her panties off.

Risa's eyes were wide and dark. Her breath came in fitful gasps as he knelt in front of her and slid his palms up her calves and thighs, firmly pushing them apart. He sensed a hesitation in her and glanced up.

"Don't," he whispered.

"Don't what?" she asked, her voice raspy.

"Be nervous. This…" he paused and gestured between them "…is something you never need to worry about."

He couldn't think, perhaps if he could, he'd notice he was in way too deep, in fact he'd crashed through every barrier he'd put up and was skidding past them. But at the moment, he didn't care. All he cared about was making sure she knew that whatever this was between them wasn't something to fear.

For a split second, her eyes flashed and then a smile curled one corner.

He slid his palm up to cup her mound, savoring the feel of her hips rolling against him. His cock throbbed, desperate to feel her around him again. But first…he slid a finger down, a soft stroke in her folds, so wet. He couldn't hold back and slipped that finger and then another into her channel, which pulsed around him as he stroked. A whimper escaped her. He finally claimed what he wanted with his mouth. She arched into him with a cry when he circled her clit with his tongue. He took his time, drugged by the sound of her pants and gasps, the evidence of her desire. He didn't stop until she cried out, arching and shuddering against him.

He moved swiftly, snatching a condom out of his jeans that lay in a rumple nearby. As he moved to shift into her, she suddenly stood and turned, shoving him down on the couch and straddling him.

"My turn," she said with a grin. Her boldness now didn't feel like a cover. She pushed him back, running her hands across his chest and down his abdomen until she reached his cock. With a light stroke, she curled a hand around his length and lifted her hips, barely coming down on him. She teased him to the point of madness, lifting and barely lowering her hips, the heated glove of her folds a taunt. Her breasts bounced softly with the motion, her nipples peaked and pink in the lamplight.

Driven beyond his endurance, the reins of his control slipped and he grabbed her hips and surged into her. Her head tipped back as she arched on a groan. Her tight wet sheath pulsed around him. He forced himself to hold still until she slowly lifted her head, her dark eyes meeting his in the shadowed room. Her lips were parted, her breath coming in soft pants. He barely managed to remain still, his cock swelling at the feel of her throbbing channel. Never breaking his gaze, he slowly shifted his hips, lifting hers incrementally, and began a circle of surges into and out of her. Her eyes flashed, her spine arched as she followed his lead, rolling her hips. Time dissolved as he lost himself in nothing but the sensation of stroking in her slick channel. Her breath became more ragged, pressure built within him. In seconds, she cried out again, clenching around him. He finally let go, his climax crashing through him as she fell against him.

With Risa's warm, soft curves plush in his lap, he came down. Their breath echoed in the quiet room. Rain fell on the roof, the sound enveloping them in the cocoon of this moment. Thought started to intrude, and Darren shoved it away. After a while, he didn't know how long since time didn't seem to exist in this space with them, he ran a hand up her back and felt goose bumps on her skin. He shifted and stood, lifting her with him. She started to wiggle out of his arms.

"Don't bother. I got you," he said softly.

She relaxed against him as he carried her into his bedroom, a room he shared with no one. He paused by the bed and met her eyes, dark and sated.

"Shower?" he asked.

With a soft smile, she nodded.

They tumbled into bed later—after a shower and a cobbled together snack of fruit and cereal. They talked about nothing much and didn't speak of what lay between them. And yet, he felt so comfortable, he didn't dare say anything aloud, for fear reality might rear its head. He fell asleep with Risa tucked against his side, her leg thrown across his and her palm on his chest.

* * *

Darren came awake with a jolt, crushing fear in his chest, barely able to catch his breath. As usual, he'd sat upright before he was fully awake. Risa's hand was on his shoulder, her eyes quietly watching him. Her features came into focus in the dark.

Oh shit. Exactly why you've made a habit of not spending the night with anyone. How the hell are you going to explain this?

He opened his mouth to say something and shut it when it occurred to him that he simply wasn't up for this. He wanted to run and erase this moment, so she didn't see him like this.

Risa's eyes were questioning, but he didn't sense that awful pity he couldn't stand. His heart rate slowed down. He tamped down the urge to jump out of bed and head for the shower.

"Are you okay?" she finally asked, her voice soft, her hand warm on his shoulder. Her thumb stroked in soft circles. His throat was tight. He had to force himself to breathe slowly.

"Yeah, yeah, I'm fine."

She waited a beat. He sensed she was giving him a chance to offer more than that, but he couldn't.

"You don't seem fine."

"Just a nightmare."

"That was some nightmare."

He couldn't help it, but he wanted to know what she meant. Because the thing was, he didn't know what happened. Before he woke, he didn't know if he thrashed or cried out. He didn't know what his nightmares looked like outside of himself. All he knew was he'd wake in a sweat, his pulse pounding and adrenaline rushing through him. If he remembered his dream, it was the same every time. Driving up to the accident, seeing the cars, breaking through the window and starting to reach for the little boy and then someone screaming his name.

"What do you mean?" he finally asked.

She shrugged, her eyes on him. "You tossed and turned for a while. That's what woke me up. You started to mumble and then hollered before you sat up like that," she said, gesturing to him. "You're covered in sweat." She slid her hand down his shoulder and arm. "Are you sure you're okay?"

He wanted to lean into her touch and shoved the thought away. Because he wasn't okay, and he damn well knew it. But he sure as hell didn't want to try to explain that to her. He'd rather find some way to escape without looking like the coward he was. But he couldn't run as fast and far as he wanted. Not now. Instead he shrugged and flung the covers back. "I'm fine, just need a quick shower."

CHAPTER 12

*R*isa slammed the door to her apartment behind her and tossed her purse and keys on the kitchen counter. One look around, and she sighed. Boxes were everywhere. She'd been bouncing between Anchorage and Diamond Creek for weeks now. She'd come up with the bright idea to pack gradually, which meant she lived half in boxes all the time. She hadn't yet figured out where she would live in Diamond Creek and was up to her eyeballs in work, so she'd been putting it off.

Every night she spent in Diamond Creek, Darren's mere existence was a magnet. She kept promising herself she'd stay with Trey and Emma, but she only managed it here and there. *It's just sex. Once the thrill wears off, you won't feel so crazy.* That's what she told herself over and over, but repetition didn't seem to be getting through to her heart. The heart she'd battened down behind a solid door was pushing against it insistently, telling her Darren was a good man and worth taking a chance on. She believed it, but she didn't believe he'd want to take a chance on her. The idea that a man like him would want her, really want her, was a foreign concept. She couldn't dare believe it and hope for more.

There was also whatever lay behind his occasional nightmares. He acted as if they were random and meant nothing, but he walled her out so completely, she knew there was something behind them. The way he behaved after the few times she'd witnessed him wake, so obviously shaken, had reinforced her plan to keep their relationship where it needed to be—on the terrain of temporary. He shut her out so thoroughly, it made her aware that no matter how she felt in his arms—so intimate it almost hurt—he wasn't open to being intimate in other ways. She couldn't help but wonder if it that had something to do with her. Though she so desperately wanted to know what lay behind the walls he'd put up around parts of himself. She wanted it so much it hurt. Which brought her full circle back to why she needed to remember to keep her heart out of this. It was clear he didn't want more, so she needed to protect herself.

A knock on her door startled her. She eyed the door, wondering who it was. She wasn't expecting anyone. She quickly flung the door open to find Brad standing there. She was so startled her mouth actually fell open. She eyed him.

"What do you want?" she asked, throwing her manners aside.

Brad attempted a smile that she assumed he meant to be contrite and endearing, but it only grated on her. Her eyes coasted over him, and she wondered how she could ever have considered him attractive. Oh, he was attractive, in the objective sense of the word, but it was so superficial. The façade had collapsed now that she knew him for who he was. He had blondish-brown hair, remarkably close to the color of Darren's. Yet what she found sexy on Darren was too carefully styled on Brad. Brad aimed for the look of someone who didn't bother with how he looked, yet he tried so hard, he couldn't quite pull it off. His blue eyes were empty to her. She didn't know what he was after, but the calculating look underneath his exterior annoyed her so much she wanted to slam the door in his face. Though his presence robbed her manners, she didn't want to make a scene.

He cleared his throat. "Can I come in?"

She shook her head firmly, crossing her arms and leaning against the door.

He nodded slowly. "Okay then. I was hoping we could move past what happened between us."

Dear God, he sounded like Gretchen. Risa sighed. "Brad, I have moved past it. It just so happens that means I don't want you in my life. I don't consider someone who lied to me as long as you did to be trustworthy, so that rules you out of the friend category. Get to the point. What do you want?"

"I don't know if you heard, but Gretchen and I broke up."

Risa kept her expression carefully blank. She hadn't heard because she'd been so busy, she hadn't paid attention to the social radar in Anchorage. Not to mention all she thought about in her spare time was Darren. She held her silence and waited.

"I was hoping maybe we could talk. I, uh, realize how things looked after what happened, but being away from you has made me realize how much you meant to me."

Risa couldn't hold her laugh back. He was so patently ridiculous. At one time, she wanted to mean something to him. Now, the idea was ludicrous, a joke she should have understood much sooner.

Brad looked affronted. "Geez, Risa. I'm trying to admit I screwed up. When you and I were together, you supported me in all the right ways and I didn't appreciate it at the time. With Gretchen, well, it's all about her..."

Risa cut him off. "And with you, it's all about you. It doesn't surprise me at all that you two blew up. It was bound to happen. But there's no way I'd reconsider anything with you. Let me guess: it's not so convenient when you lose all my connections around here, and Ethan and Jack are cutting you out of your coveted arts committees and what-not. Brad, forget it. If there's one thing I learned from you, it's that I should have seen you for what you were much sooner. Don't come by, don't call. I wish you the best."

At that, Risa stepped back and quietly shut the door in Brad's face, bolting it and walking away. She heard him call her name through the door a few times before footsteps headed away from her door down the hall. Kicking a box out of the way, she collapsed on the couch. The flash of annoyance with Brad faded quickly. She felt strangely calm. Instead of being embarrassed to see him, the clarity she felt about him was refreshing.

Darren was everything Brad wasn't—genuine, unassuming, and sexy in that down-to-earth, rugged way that slipped right under her defenses and set her on fire. And dammit, she didn't want to make a fool of herself over him. With Brad, now that the freshness of his betrayal had faded, she could look back and laugh because she didn't want someone like him. She'd meant it when she'd told Gretchen she'd done her a favor. But with Darren...letting him matter would mean a much deeper scar. At first, she'd been afraid because he might have duped her as Brad had. The more she got to know him, the more it became apparent he was good—hold on and not let go kind of good. And she didn't know if she was good enough for him. That problem was an impossible one to fix. She stood abruptly and headed for the kitchen to scrounge up dinner.

DARREN STOOD in front of his refrigerator wondering what the hell to eat. The sparse contents reminded him of the last night Risa had been here. He discovered she often wanted to snack after their bouts of earth-shattering sex. She teased him over the past weekend that he needed to find a personal shopper since he so rarely had much in the house when it came to food. With a sigh, he snatched the milk out and grabbed a box of cereal from the cabinet. Suddenly, there was a sharp knock at his door. Before he took more than three steps, the door flew open.

His sister, Hallie, came through the door in a whirl, her arms laden with bags.

"Darren!"

Hallie set her bags down and ran over to hug him. She moved so quickly he hadn't managed to swallow the bite of cereal in his mouth until she stepped away. She was dressed in black leggings with a bright blue button-down flannel shirt. Her soft brown hair was tied in a knot on the top of her head. She smiled expectantly at him, her hazel eyes tilting at the corners.

"Hey Hallie. How's it going?"

Her smile wobbled.

"You okay?"

The smile completely disappeared and tears welled in her eyes.

Darren didn't know what was going on, but he had enough sense to set his bowl of cereal on the counter and walk her to the couch to sit down.

At which point, Hallie burst into tears. His little sister, who he adored, crying sent his heart in his throat, and a flash of protectiveness clenched like a vice inside. He floundered as he watched her sobbing.

"Hallie, what's going on?"

She rubbed her eyes and sighed. "You remember Ryan?"

Darren nodded. "The guy you followed to Greece because you were in love and had to follow your heart?"

Hallie nodded, the misery in her eyes making it clear that Ryan had wiped away the carefree joy Hallie was blessed to carry with her. That made Darren instantly angry, but he held back and waited.

"I'm such an idiot. Ryan...well, we got to Greece and things were okay for a little while and then I found out he had some other girlfriend on the side. And then when I got into an argument with him about it, he..." Hallie paused and looked at Darren carefully.

Darren didn't know what she was about to say, but he could tell she was concerned about how he'd respond. If there was one thing he and Hallie had always had, it was honesty. Their parents, though loving, had been committed to their careers. Their father worked long hours as an investigative cop while their mother threw herself into her academic career. He and Hallie took care of each other while their parents' minds were focused elsewhere. It wasn't a bad childhood, but it had formed a strong bond between them.

"He threw me out!" Hallie said forcefully and promptly burst into tears again.

"Okay, and then what happened?" he asked, his quiet words belying how he felt inside. Picturing Hallie all alone in Greece after the man who persuaded her to follow him left her to fend for herself infuriated him. He wanted to slam his fist into the man's face, but that wasn't exactly an option at the moment what with him here in Alaska, and Ryan in Greece. He silently vowed if he ever laid eyes on Ryan again, he would have the satisfaction of one good slug. He closed his eyes, clenching his jaw, and forced himself to breath slowly. His fury would do Hallie little good.

Hallie rubbed her sleeve across her face and took a breath. "Well, first he started swearing and told me I didn't have any right to tell him who he could be with. He just went on and on. He finally left and said I had to be gone before he got back. I packed everything and left right then. But I don't have much money saved up and don't know where to go. I don't want to tell Mom and Dad. They'll just think I'm an idiot. Dad already said I needed to stop being so flighty and even though he didn't say anything about it, I know he thought Ryan was a loser. Of course, he had to be right. So I came here..." Her words trailed off and she shrugged. "Can I stay here for a little bit until I figure out what to do?"

Darren didn't hesitate. "Of course. Did you drive here from Anchorage?"

"Yeah. I had a return ticket and I was able to change the date. I sold my car before I left, so I rented one and drove straight here. I'll have to return it tomorrow to the airport in Homer though. I can't afford another day. I just need a little time to get some work somewhere and figure out what to do."

The wheels in Darren's mind spun. He wanted to grill her with more questions about Ryan. Well, to be specific, he wanted to hop on a plane, fly to Greece and satisfy his urge to punch the guy. Since that wasn't an option, he glanced at Hallie, trying to assess how she was doing.

"Is there anything else that happened with Ryan?"

She shook her head. "No. I just wanted to be gone. And don't go all big-brother on me. Yeah, he was a total ass, but I guess it's better I figured that out sooner rather than later. I'm not going back. I don't ever want to see him again."

Darren didn't really give a damn that Hallie warned him against going big-brother, but he was relieved to know she didn't want to see Ryan again.

Darren nodded. "I'll leave it alone for now, but I reserve the right to give the guy a piece of my mind and then some if I ever see him. You're also calling mom and dad tonight to let them know you're here. I don't want them worrying about where you are."

Hallie fiddled with her hair, untying the knot so that it fell around her shoulders. "Okay, I'll call them in a little bit." She slanted her eyes at him and wrinkled her nose. "I've dumped my sob story on you.

Now tell me what's up with you and who that pretty blue scarf belongs to? Because I know damn well it doesn't belong to you, so don't even bother trying to pretend it does." She gestured to a scarf hanging on the back of one of the stools by the kitchen counter.

Risa had left it here. He chuckled before replying. "I might be seeing someone."

Hallie squealed and clapped her hands. "Really? Oh Darren, that makes me so happy. You are the best brother in the world and the best kind of guy! I keep hoping some woman will snatch you up and hold on for dear life." She paused, her gaze sobering. Hallie knew how much he'd struggled after the accident and his guilt over not being able to get that little boy out in time. Hallie probably knew more than anyone, but he'd never explicitly told her he'd thought he might avoid relationships for the long haul. So this thing with Risa...well, it was a *thing*.

"Does that mean you're sleeping better at night?" Hallie asked softly.

Darren flushed and nodded. "Most of the time. Not all the time."

He'd told Hallie how awful it had been to see the pity in Jill's eyes the few times she'd stayed with him before they broke up. He thought back to the other night when he woke to see Risa watching him. Discomfort roiled inside. *You like her too much. It's getting dangerous. If she gets too close, she'll look at you the way Jill did.*

He couldn't let his mind go there now, so he focused on Hallie. She twirled a lock of hair around her finger and eyed him thoughtfully. She appeared to sense he didn't want to talk further about his sleeping, or anything to do with why he hadn't been in a relationship in so long. Her eyes took on a gleam. "So, do I get to meet this mysterious woman?"

Darren grinned. "As if I could avoid it."

Hallie squealed again and stood quickly. "Okay, what do you have to eat? I'm ready to hear all about her. Starting with her name."

CHAPTER 13

"No, we need to repaint the whole gallery!" Ethan declared.

Jack rolled his eyes. "And who will be doing all this painting?"

Ethan shrugged and took a sip of wine. "I'm sure Risa can find someone to do it, right dear?"

Risa arched a brow and glanced between them. "I'm sure I can. The question is do you want to spend that much money on painting? As it is, the gallery has basic bland cream-colored walls. Nothing to distract from the artwork we put in there. I'll let you two sort this one out."

They were at dinner in Anchorage, deep into planning for the gallery in Diamond Creek. Ethan and Jack enjoyed bantering over business decisions such as this. When she'd first worked for them, she wanted to problem solve these kinds of decisions. But then she realized they enjoyed tussling over details, so she left them to their own devices.

Jack grinned at her and turned to Ethan. "Precisely

my point. There's no reason to waste the money on painting. Not to mention it also means we'd have to clear everything out for the painters. Too much work."

Ethan rolled his eyes and didn't bother holding back his return grin. With an elegant shrug of his suited shoulders, he turned to her. "You just had to go and support him."

Risa giggled. "You know that's not what I meant. I pointed out the situation and nothing more. Moving on, do you have a firm date in mind yet for the opening?"

They enthusiastically moved on to concrete planning details. The last few weeks had flown by. Ethan and Jack had closed on the sale of the gallery in Diamond Creek. Meanwhile, she'd been working with them on selecting and ordering artwork for the gallery. She'd been back and forth to Diamond Creek almost every week, spending most nights with Darren when she was there. Her schedule was such a whirlwind she managed to keep her mind in a blissful bubble where she didn't think too much about the depth of feelings he elicited. Once in a while, reality nudged her and her fear that she was letting him mean too much would start to overwhelm her. With so much to do, she'd force her mind away and ignore her worries.

In the midst of all this, she was still packing up her apartment box by box without a firm plan of where she'd be staying in Diamond Creek. Trey and Emma had offered to let her stay with them indefinitely. She likely would start there, but she didn't want to make that more than a very temporary situation. Back when Trey's first wife had died, Risa had moved in to help out with Stuart for a while. But now that Trey was settled again, she wanted them to be the family they were without her being smack in the middle day in and day out. Not to mention that staying with them might bring up a few questions about Darren—questions she wasn't quite ready to face.

Because you have every intention of spending plenty of time with him. And what exactly does that mean? It means I can't keep my hands off of him and he's the best thing that ever happened to me. Oh see, that right there, that's why you need to wake up and pay attention. You can't pretend he's nothing more than a casual fling for much longer. Because you know damn well he's not. You're already in too deep, and he's way too good for you.

Risa's internal back and forth was interrupted when Ethan said her name.

"What?" she asked.

He glanced to Jack with a grin. "She's daydreaming about Darren again."

Her face felt hot. "I am not!" She internally justified this with the argument that while she'd been thinking about Darren, it wasn't a daydream. Daydreaming was what she'd been doing earlier while on hold with one of their suppliers. To be specific, she'd been remembering what it felt like when Darren slid his palms up her thighs, the calloused skin sending shivers through her body, just before his thumbs reached the juncture of her thighs and he caressed the wet heat that was ever-present when he was near. She flushed deeper when Jack cleared his throat.

Her eyes flew up and met Jack's warm, kind blue gaze. He shrugged and shook his head. Ethan chuckled before his eyes sobered.

"I was teasing, you know," he said softly.

"I know."

Ethan gave her a considering look. "All joking aside, how are things with Darren? Don't even bother trying to pretend you're not seeing him."

Risa sighed and took a quick gulp of wine for fortitude. "I won't do that. You know I tell you two just about everything. Things are…way too good, and I'm not sure what any of it means. I didn't want this to be serious, and I don't think it is. But I don't know what to do, or where things are going."

Jack pursed his lips. "Well, what's he saying?"

"We don't exactly talk much." The blush that had finally faded returned with a vengeance.

Ethan and Jack both grinned.

"So that's how it is then," Ethan commented before turning to Jack. "You didn't get a chance to meet Darren, but I told you my gut said he was a good one for our girl."

Risa crossed and uncrossed her legs. She knew Ethan to have remarkably accurate assessments of people, so if he had a good feeling about Darren, it meant a lot to her. She'd brushed off his dismissal of Brad when she'd first started dating Brad. He'd turned out to be spot on as he'd described Brad as shallow, superficial, and interested only in what served his purposes. At the time, she'd been offended when now she wished she'd had enough sense to listen. What frightened her about his gut when it came to Darren was she didn't know if she could live up to the kind of woman Darren deserved. Not to mention that Darren seemed to carry some of his own baggage, namely whatever lay behind his occasional nightmares. She wished she knew what was behind them…and wished he would confide in her.

She glanced to Ethan. "So you think he's a good one then?"

"I already told you that. You're fishing, but I'll bite. I like Darren. He's quiet, but he's steady and you need that. He also clearly adores you though he tries to play it cool. And then there's the fact that he's pure eye candy, all muscly, smoldering and unassuming." Ethan caught Jack's eye. "If I wasn't so in love with you, I might be tempted."

Jack threw back his head in a laugh, and Risa kicked Ethan under the table. "He's not even your type! You said he was too manly for you."

Ethan shrugged. "In my younger days, I was known to push out of my comfort zone. That's what you need to do. Since I've known you, your comfort zone is casual, but not because you want it that way. Because you don't dare hope for something more," he said, his eyes sobering abruptly.

Risa felt his words ping in her center. She swallowed and looked away, tears pricking in her eyes. As usual, Ethan didn't shy away from anything uncomfortable. Her skin prickled with the discomfort of how close he hit home with his comment. That's how she kept her heart safe—not hoping for something more. With Darren, she was desperate for more and could hardly stand to think about it. When she gathered herself and turned back, Ethan lifted his wineglass. "You know I only want you to get what you deserve, right?"

She cleared her throat, his warm smile easing her heart. "I know," she replied softly.

* * *

RISA CRESTED the top of the hill that dipped down to Diamond Creek. She was on her way to Darren's house. She'd driven down from Anchorage after work this evening, and it was getting late. Once she came over the hill, Kachemak Bay unfurled in the view, the water rippling in the setting sun. Shafts of pink and dusty gold fell across the mountains. The lights at Otter Cove Harbor came on as she drove toward town, the harbor lighting up like a postcard. She opened her windows and let the ocean air swirl through the car, inhaling deeply. The crisp, salty scent invigorated her.

Moments later, she pulled up at Darren's house. As she closed her car door, she realized he'd likely get a chuckle out of the fact that she was driving yet another car. Her first replacement after her accident had bit the dust when her engine overheated. The mechanic had kindly informed her he could fix it, but the cost was steeper than she preferred. Now she had another used car, an allegedly reliable Toyota. With her luck lately, it would be the opposite of reliable, but one could hope. She slung her bag over her shoulder and strode to the door. With a sharp knock, she opened it and walked in to find a woman who looked to be roughly her own age standing at the kitchen counter. The woman was stirring something in a bowl and turned away to wipe her hands on a towel. She didn't seem to have noticed Risa.

"Hey Darren, when did you say Risa was getting here?" the woman asked, appearing to assume Risa was Darren.

Risa cleared her throat. "Risa's here," she offered.

The woman whirled around, dishtowel in hand. She promptly flung it on the counter and squealed. "Oh my God! You're here!" She raced over and hugged Risa before stepping back with a wide smile on her face. She was close to Risa in height with a slight build, soft brown hair tied in a knot with a pen stuck through it, and warm hazel eyes. Risa was disoriented to find a beautiful young woman clearly at home in Darren's house. Before she could formulate a thought beyond her confusion and a flash of fear that she'd been completely wrong about Darren and he was seeing someone else, the woman spoke.

"I'm Hallie, Darren's sister. I'm soooo happy to meet you."

Risa's brain clicked. Of course, Darren had mentioned the other night on the phone his sister was in town, but he didn't know how long she'd be here. She was clearly still here.

"Oh hi! Darren mentioned you were visiting. It's nice to meet you," Risa replied, her mind whirring. Her valiant efforts to keep Darren in a casual corner in her brain bumped against what her heart wanted— to let go and see what kind of chance they might have. Meeting his sister made things seem…not so casual. She alternately wanted to make her excuses and leave, or pick Hallie's brain for everything she knew about Darren, so Risa could learn what made him tick.

Hallie beamed and reached over to take Risa's bag. "Here, let me get that." She set it on the couch and tucked her hand into Risa's elbow. "Come sit with me while I finish up. I was making dinner for you and Darren. I had this whole sneaky plan that I'd have it ready before you got here, but he wasn't sure about the timing."

Bemused with Hallie's enthusiasm, Risa gamely followed her to the kitchen counter, sliding onto one of the stools beside it. "Well, when he asked what time I'd be here, I didn't really know, so there was no way he'd know. You're making us dinner?"

Hallie grinned, her hazel eyes tilting up when she did. "If you haven't noticed, Darren's not exactly much of a food guy. He loves good food, but he can never be bothered to shop well or take time to cook. When I found out about you, I wanted to surprise you for him. But it's okay you're earlier than I thought. We can chat before Darren gets here. So tell me everything."

Risa couldn't help but return Hallie's grin. Hallie was a bundle of warmth, sweetness and spunk. "What's everything?"

Hallie's grin didn't fade, but her eyes sobered slightly. "Okay, here's the thing: Darren's my one and only big brother, and I love him to pieces. He's there for me whenever I need him, and he's a great guy. But he hardly ever dates and I would love for him to find someone. I mean, he's a catch! Right?"

Risa's heart thumped…hard. Darren was the kind of man a woman wanted, the catch Hallie described. She wanted to be the one who managed to hold onto him, and she just didn't know if he felt the same way about her. To add to his list of virtues, he clearly had a great relationship with his sister. She forced herself to focus on Hallie and nodded.

At Risa's nod, Hallie's grin widened before she continued. "So when he mentioned you, I got so excited. You might think I'm meddling, but I don't mean to." When Risa raised her brows, Hallie threw her hands up. "I guess I am! I just want to make sure you know how awesome my brother is."

Risa's heart clenched. She knew quite well how awesome Darren was, and that all the good things about him extended far beyond how amazing he was in bed. She looked over at Hallie's earnest face. "You don't need to do any convincing. I've already figured out how awesome Darren is," she said with a soft smile. "So what are we having for dinner?"

Hallie beamed again. "I made a salmon casserole that's already in the oven and just finished stirring the salad dressing I made to go with the salad."

"You made the dressing?"

"Yup. A raspberry vinaigrette. I love to cook, so when Darren told me you'd be here, I was all over it. I'm headed out to have dinner with a friend who moved down here a few years ago. We're going to have a girls' night, so you and Darren have the place to yourselves."

"Oh, you don't have to steer clear on my account." Risa was genuinely enjoying Hallie's company, though it was hard to think about anything other than having Darren all to herself. The back and forth between Anchorage and Diamond Creek only gave her glimpses of Darren, so she was constantly hungering for more time with him.

Hallie shook her head. "Yes I do. I don't want to prevent any opportunities for romance. Having one's sister around isn't exactly romantic," she said wryly. She quickly tugged a funnel out of a drawer and proceeded to carefully pour the salad dressing into a small glass bottle.

Risa had so many questions she wanted to ask, but

wasn't certain it was okay. Hallie glanced up and caught her expression. "Ask me anything."

A laugh bubbled up. "Anything?"

Hallie shrugged. "I'll tell you what I can. It's obvious to me Darren likes you…a lot."

Risa's heart jumped, and a flush warmed her. Much as she was trying to convince herself they were just having a fling—a smoking hot fling—the feeling between them teetered on the edge of something much bigger than she'd ever contemplated. With Hallie's openness, she decided to dive in.

"Did you know he has nightmares sometimes?"

Hallie's gaze sobered. She nodded and rinsed the funnel before putting it in the dishwasher. She leaned her hips against the counter and tilted her head. "So he still has nightmares then?"

"Not often, but enough that I wondered about it."

Hallie took a deep breath and eyed Risa for a long moment. "Did he tell you anything about why he left Seattle?"

"He mentioned he had enough of the city cop thing, but that's about it."

Hallie nodded slowly. "That's one way to put it. I wish Darren would tell you what happened, but I'm not so sure he will. He never asked me to keep it a secret, so I don't mind telling you. Do me a favor and give him a little time on this one, okay?"

Risa's curiosity lunged, but she nodded. Watching him wake scared and rattled in the night tugged at her. Any opportunity to understand him better was too tempting to turn down.

"Darren was the first on the scene at a bad accident on the interstate. He was in the middle of trying to get a little boy out of one of the cars when it exploded. Everyone in the car died, including the little boy. They said afterwards that the little boy's parents died of injuries from the impact before the car went up in flames, but the little boy was alive when Darren got there. He was in his car seat and alert according to the witnesses. Darren got lucky and came away with some cuts on his face and temporary lung injury due to the massive heat from the smoke. To this day, I know he feels guilty, like he somehow should have moved faster. But no one else was there to help yet, and everyone said he did all he could to get that little boy out. He doesn't like to talk about it. They had him see a therapist afterwards to help him with what he was going through. He had a lot of trouble sleeping at first. For weeks, I don't know if he slept more than a few hours a night. After he moved here, he told me he finally got a better handle on his sleep. But he's hardly dated since the accident."

Risa's throat tightened. Her heart ached for Darren. She knew something like that would haunt him. He was so good-hearted and always wanted to help. Though it was obvious there was nothing he could have done differently, she knew the accident would linger for him. She looked over at Hallie whose eyes watched her carefully.

"That's terrible," Risa said softly. "Now I understand why he still has nightmares sometimes. He acts like they're nothing. I wish…" She wished she could make it better. All he could do was learn to live with it and try to somehow believe there was nothing else he could have done. She thought about how he handled the situation with Eric after he bumped into her car that afternoon. He was kind and funny, and he made sure Eric was held accountable without it being anything more than it needed to be. She thought about the times they went to dinner in town, and he fielded frequent inquiries from people, clearly well-liked and respected by most everyone in town. She remembered that Trey thought the world of him for how he helped Emma with her abusive ex. The man who was all of those things to so many people would be heartbroken over a little boy dying and thinking he could have done something to prevent it. That was part of the problem—he was so competent in so many ways, it would be hard for him to convince himself he couldn't have done more, no matter what the facts demonstrated. She was relieved to understand what lay behind his nightmares, but it hurt a little that he couldn't confide in her.

Risa met Hallie's gaze again. "Thank you for explaining. I'm pretty sure I'd have gotten far fewer details from him. I won't bring it up unless he does, but I can't tell you how much it means to understand. He's only had a few nightmares, but the look on his face when he wakes up is so sad."

Hallie nodded. "I know. I stayed with him for a few days when he got out of the hospital."

They sat quietly for a few moments. Risa glanced out the windows. The sun had almost fallen behind the mountains with a half-moon rising through the dusky sky. The moon cast a soft beam of light across the water, the waves glittering in its path. A stellar jay flew past the windows and landed on the deck railing, barely visible in the fading light. It called sharply, a raven answering in the distance. She thought about what Hallie told her and what it illuminated about Darren. If she'd wondered if she was succeeding at keeping her feelings light, she knew with certainty she'd failed completely. She wanted to soothe the ache she knew he held in his heart over this. *That's not exactly casual. I know...and I don't care.*

Risa turned back to Hallie. "I'm not sure what to say now."

Hallie shrugged. "That was pretty heavy. But I'm glad I told you because now I know Darren matters to you," she said with a sly grin.

Risa threw her head back in a laugh. "Am I that obvious?"

Hallie nodded vigorously before her gaze sobered again. "Seriously, I'd rather you know than have Darren tell you only half the story. You need to know the whole picture. Now let's move on to lighter matters. Darren said you manage an art gallery in Anchorage and that you're helping get one started here."

They moved on to discussing Risa's work, and when Darren arrived later, Risa's breath caught when he walked in. He looked just delicious in his uniform. His velvety brown eyes caressed her when he approached the kitchen counter.

"So I see Hallie let you in," he said with a grin.

Before Risa could reply, Hallie chimed in. "Of course I did! And dinner's ready."

Darren tugged Hallie close for a quick hug. "Thanks Hallie." He caught Risa's eyes. "She insisted on this dinner thing. She seems to think I don't do the best job around the kitchen," he said with an abashed shrug.

Hallie swatted him with the kitchen towel. "You're terrible at taking care of yourself." She wrinkled her nose and grinned at him as she stepped away, hanging the kitchen towel on the oven handle. "I have no shame. I freely told Risa I wanted you two to have a nice dinner, and that I was all about doing my best to make sure she realized how awesome you are."

Darren shook his head and flushed slightly. Risa felt a little thrill to know that perhaps he wanted to impress her. Hallie strode to the door and grabbed her purse and a jacket off the coat rack by the door. "I'm off for the night. I'll see you two tomorrow."

"Hallie, no one's pushing you out all night," Darren called out.

Hallie paused with her hand on the doorknob. "Oh, I know. But you two need the place to yourselves." At that, she swung the door open and left. A second later, the door opened again and Hallie's smiling face came around the corner. "I'm borrowing your car, okay?"

Darren chuckled. "I figured. Keys are in it."

Hallie blew a kiss and was gone in a whirl.

CHAPTER 14

Risa woke in the dark. Darren had cried out in his sleep again. She rolled to her side. Her eyes gradually adjusted to the dark, and she could see his chest rise and fall rapidly. She reached a hand over, carefully touching his shoulder. Suddenly, his whole body jerked and his eyes flew open on a loud breath. He lay completely still for a long moment before slowly turning his head toward her. She kept her hand still on his shoulder, trying to soothe him without words. Now that she knew what lay behind the dreams, it viscerally pained her to see him like this. His skin was damp under her touch. He tended to wake up covered in sweat when this happened. The room was quiet save for his ragged breathing, which gradually slowed. Moonlight fell in a shaft through the skylight above the bed.

Darren cleared his throat. "Mind if I take a shower?" he asked, his voice gravelly.

She shook her head. Though he'd only had these nightmares a few times when she was with him, she'd come to know he showered afterward and figured it helped somehow. She knew if she were him, she'd feel better after a shower, if anything, to wash the heat of the dream away. A tiny corner of her heart wished he'd talk to her about how he felt, wished he would let her help him feel better.

He rolled off the bed and strode to the bathroom adjacent to his bedroom. She rested against the pillows and watched the stars above while she waited. When he returned moments later, he climbed in bed and lay on his back. He'd left the bathroom light on and soft light spilled in an angle across the bed. She curled on her side and placed her hand on his chest. He tensed. His heart thudded against her palm. She hadn't meant it to, but desire slid through her, curling like smoke around them. She leaned on her elbow and looked at him. His features were sharp in the darkened room. The lines of his strong jaw and sensual lips a temptation. There was just enough light for her to see the scar on the side of his face, the one she'd wondered about until Hallie told her about it last night. It ran in a faded, jagged path from his upper cheekbone and disappeared into his hairline above his ear. She traced it softly with the tip of her finger. Her pulse raced, butterflies clustered in her belly. Though she wasn't certain what he thought, his heart pounding under her palm told her he felt something. She shifted and twined her leg over his, her thigh brushing against his arousal. The heat from him flashed through her.

In those dark hours of the early morning when night still held them in its grip, she wanted to take him inside of her and make him remember he was here now and that whatever visited his dreams from time to time was but a memory. A corner of her mind, the one that kept her heart well and protected, had something to say. But for now, she didn't care to hear. The want stretched inside and spread its wings. Full-fledged desire flew through her—a desire girded with a depth of feeling she couldn't examine just now.

She rose up, shimmying out of her underwear as she did, and straddled him. In one motion, she tugged the t-shirt she wore up and over her head. It drifted down through the path of light and fell to the floor. His shaft was hot and hard against her through his briefs. She shifted her hips and pressed down briefly. She met his eyes, dark in the shadowed light. He lifted a hand, grazing the back of it against her belly and the soft curves of her breasts. Her breath caught, sensation spiraling through her at the brush of his touch. He flattened his palm in between her breasts, his thumb caressing a nipple as he held her gaze. Not a word passed between them. Risa felt electrified.

She shifted up and tugged his briefs down, hooking them with her foot to pull them off his legs. She paused to look at him. He'd propped himself on his elbows when she moved. The hard planes of his chest were shadowed. His body was a sight to behold —all muscle and burnished skin catching the light that angled across the bed. His arousal was blatant. Though the intimacy she felt with him bordered on terrifying for her at moments, she gloried in it. With a soft smile, she leaned forward and took him in her mouth. His breath escaped in a groan.

She brought him fully into her mouth before dragging back up, savoring the salty taste of his skin. She angled to the side to stroke her tongue up and down. His head tipped back and his chest rose and fell with deep breaths. She cupped him in her hand, alternating between her mouth and hand, shivering when she tasted his pre-cum on her tongue.

"*Risa...*"

"*Mmmm...*" *she hummed around his cock.*

"*Come here...please...*"

She couldn't find it in her to deny him. She also ached to have him inside of her. With a last stroke, she rose and straddled him again. He reached over to the nightstand where she knew he kept condoms. But now, tonight, she wanted to feel him fully.

"I'm on the pill," she whispered.

He froze and turned his head back to her, his eyes inscrutable. "Risa, you don't have to…"

"I know I don't have to. But I'm on the pill. I have been for years. I'm clean. I can promise you that, and I know you are too. Because that's how you are. I just want to feel you…" She paused and shrugged, self-consciousness starting to flood through her.

Darren fell back against the pillows, his eyes boring into hers. "Don't think," he said softly. He tugged her forward, reaching a hand between them to stroke into her folds. She was drenched in desire and couldn't help from pressing her hips into his hand, desperate for his touch. She bit her lip and groaned when he slid two fingers in a deep thrust inside, his thumb circling her clit. When his hand moved away, she whimpered and then gasped when he dragged the head of his cock back and forth through her slick moisture. In a swift move, he surged into her.

She threw her head back and arched up before sinking her hips onto him completely. He held her hips with one hand as she established a rhythm with him. Pleasure suffused her as he stroked in and out of her, filling her completely again and again and again. She raced to the delicious edge and tumbled over, her climax rippling through her. He gasped her name in a final surge and slid his palm up her back swiftly, tugging her against his chest. She tucked her face into his neck, trying to catch her breath. Their hearts thudded against each other. He threaded a hand in her hair and softly stroked through it.

Risa lay against Darren and wondered if she could keep her heart protected. It was becoming more and more apparent that she might have already lost the battle she'd been fighting. Darren simply slipped inside her heart before she knew it. And now, with the beat of his heart echoing against her ear, it felt so *right* to be with him. In this moment, she didn't have it in her to wrestle with her feelings. The cool air caused her skin to pebble as the heat of their passion faded. She shifted, lifting up and off of him. Before she could move away, Darren tugged her close, molding her against his side and tucking the quilt around them. "Don't go anywhere," he said gruffly.

"I wasn't planning to," she protested.

"Oh, I didn't think you were going somewhere literally. I didn't want you to scoot away from me," he said with a soft chuckle.

She couldn't help but giggle and settled against him. Several moments later, his palm, which had been idly stroking her back fell still, and the rhythm of his breathing told her he'd fallen asleep. She smiled against his shoulder. This was the first time he'd fallen asleep with her after one of his nightmares. Her heart trilled at what that might mean.

*D*arren pulled his jacket on before heading out to the parking lot. Summer weather had blown away with the winds of fall. A brisk wind gusted off the bay. Clouds coasted across the sky, shadows coming and going against the mountains as the clouds passed in front of the sun. He drove out of the parking lot to head home. His mind filled with thoughts of Risa, as appeared to be the case whenever he didn't have something to keep him focused. She was back in Anchorage packing and working on the gallery planning. From what she told him, she'd be in Diamond Creek full time within the next few weeks. He could tell she was tired and working herself too hard between getting organized to move herself and the planning for the gallery.

He couldn't help the spark of anticipation every time he thought about the reality of her being here every day. This was predictably followed with a flash of discomfort. Risa had somehow seeped through the cracks of his defenses. He could hardly stand to think about the other night when he woke after another nightmare. She didn't shy away, yet she didn't make much of it. With a touch and her mere presence, she'd wiped the slate of his mind clean. Instead of his usual pattern of lying awake, ruminating after he showered, he'd fallen into the spell she wove around them. Deep within, he was tiptoeing around what it meant that she'd stayed with him through to the other side of his nightmares. She'd managed what he thought was impossible—to take his mind to another place. Hope was sprouting in the cracks of his defenses. And damn if he knew what to do about it.

He shook his head to clear it and turned into his driveway to find Jared Winters climbing into his truck. Jared grinned and stepped back out when Darren pulled up.

"Hey there. Just stopping by to see if you want to go fishing sometime soon. We're finally slowing down," Jared said by way of greeting when Darren stepped out of his patrol car.

Darren leaned against the car and nodded. "Would love to. It's been so busy this summer, I've only managed to get out fishing a few times. I haven't seen you since Susie had the baby. Congratulations, by the way. I tried to stop by a few times, but missed you each time."

Jared's return smile was proud. "I got your messages. No worry there. Susie and Patrick are doing great. We've had so much company, I think she's about ready to kick everyone out," he said with a chuckle. "How've you been?"

Darren shrugged. "Busy but good. Just like you guys, summer keeps me running. My sister's been staying with me for a bit."

"I know. She introduced herself when I showed up. She tells me you're dating Risa Holden," Jared said with a sly smile.

Darren groaned and shook his head.

"Does that mean Hallie's wrong and you're not dating Risa?" Jared asked, arching a brow.

Darren sighed and rolled his eyes. "I didn't say that. Just shaking my head about Hallie. I have been seeing Risa here and there," he said, wishing he didn't need to explain anything. It wasn't that he was trying to hide anything, but more that he didn't know how to define what they were doing.

Jared nodded slowly. "Hmm. Don't suppose Trey knows you two are seeing each other?"

Darren groaned again. "Don't know if he does. It's not..." he trailed off, not sure how to explain what Risa was to him and bothered that it may appear he was trying to hide something when he wasn't.

Jared's eyes sharpened with a knowing look. "You look like a man who's gone a step further than he planned to go. I'm guessing you haven't seen Risa much since she lives in Anchorage, but somehow she's gotten under your skin. Am I right?"

Darren rolled his head side to side, trying to ease the tension in his neck. He didn't see Jared too much, but he was a good friend. It wouldn't hurt to bounce this off of him. He flushed thinking about it, but made himself talk anyway. "Under my skin is one way to put it. Honestly, I don't know how the hell this happened. I met her and thought she was beautiful. Next thing I know, I've seen her a few times between here and Anchorage, and I can't seem to keep my head straight. And before you go thinking I've been hiding something, I haven't. We haven't even seen each other all that much, it's just..." *She's slipped right inside and you don't even know what to do about it. You think you can keep her in a tidy corner, but you haven't been able to since the day you met her. You are in deep.* His mind taunted him.

Jared held his gaze. "Just what?"

Darren took a breath. Risa sauntered through his mind—her dark brown hair and eyes, her sensual mouth and lush body, her quick wit, her endearing combination of bold and reserved...and that vulnerable side to her she tried so hard to hide. If he let himself think about it, all he wanted was to be with her. The simple truth was he'd made a decision *not* to let that kind of intimacy into his life because it meant opening the door to his own heart and facing the potential that she'd see how broken he felt. But Risa... she walked right through his guard without even trying.

"I think I can answer my own question," Jared said wryly.

Darren whipped his head up to find Jared eyeing him with a rueful grin.

"What do you mean?" Darren asked.

"I know that look because I've been there. Next question is what are you gonna do about it?"

Fear flashed through him. Before he could respond, Jared did. "Okay then, should I shut up about now?"

Darren's brain kicked back in gear. "You don't need to shut up. I need to get a grip."

Jared shrugged. "Or maybe not. Maybe you're getting in your own way."

Jared was so close to the truth, it made Darren want to squirm. But he trusted Jared's opinion, and he prided himself on not being a coward, so he held his gaze and took a breath. "Maybe so. Any suggestions?"

"Don't think so hard. And don't let a good thing pass you by because it seems more comfortable not to deal with it. I almost did, so I know the feeling."

Jared's words hit so close to home that Darren almost flinched. He considered the idea of Risa passing him by and felt hollow at the mere thought. He met Jared's eyes and nodded slowly. "Okay. I'll, uh, try not to do that."

Jared grinned and pushed away from his truck. "So what's a good day for fishing next week?"

"How about Wednesday?"

"I'll call you the day before to confirm. Never know what the weather might do between now and then."

CHAPTER 16

Risa hefted another box into the moving truck and brushed her hair out of her face. Ethan and Jack had made arrangements for her to share space in the delivery truck transporting inventory to Diamond Creek for the gallery. Her apartment was almost empty, and she was exhausted. She trudged back upstairs and did a quick walk through to see if there were any leftover boxes. When she came back into the living room, Ethan was leaning against the wall, looking immaculate and dapper in a crisp white shirt and navy slacks. She felt dusty and dirty in comparison in her torn jeans and faded t-shirt, her hair tugged into a messy ponytail.

"Hello there," Ethan said before wagging his finger at her. "You're not supposed to be carting boxes around. That was the point of us hiring the moving crew. There's an entire crew of strong, sexy men to carry things for you. I show up and they tell me you won't listen to them."

Before Risa could reply, one of the men in question strode through the door. As Ethan pointed out, he was strong and sexy, a bit brawny for Risa's taste, but nonetheless. He towered over Ethan as he smiled down at him. He adjusted the baseball hat he wore. "I think we're about done. Just so you know, we tried to get her to stop carrying boxes…"

Ethan cut him off. "No need to apologize. I'm well aware of how stubborn she can be. Thank you for trying. What time will the truck arrive in Diamond Creek tomorrow?"

"We're estimating we'll be there by ten or eleven in the morning. That should give us plenty of time."

Ethan nodded. "We'll meet you there." With a handshake and a nod at Risa, the man left.

Ethan tilted his head to the side. "You're staying with us tonight, right?"

"Let me grab my bag, and we can get out of here."

Risa checked the bathroom quickly to make sure she hadn't left anything and swung the single bag she'd packed with a few days worth of clothes and toiletries. She'd already dropped her laptop and some other items at their place this morning before the movers arrived.

A short drive later, and she walked into Ethan and Jack's comfortable home on the outskirts of Anchorage on the hillside south of town. They lived in a sleek, modern timber frame home. It was, of course, beautifully decorated. For this moment, it was unfortunate that the couch and chairs in the living room were white because Risa didn't dare sit down. At Jack's wave, she headed to the guest suite for a shower. Feeling much better after a shower and change of clothes, she returned shortly and joined Jack on a stool at the kitchen counter.

Ethan passed her a plate of pasta with a lemon garlic olive oil sauce while Jack poured her a glass of wine. They chatted quietly while she ate. When she pushed her plate away, Jack met her gaze.

"Ethan tells me you still don't know where you're staying when you get to Diamond Creek."

Risa canted her eyes to Ethan. "What is it with you and making sure you know all my plans?"

Ethan shrugged. "It's what friends do. It's perfectly fine for you to plan to stay with Trey and Emma, but I find it interesting that you keep hedging when I ask."

Jack chuckled. "Interesting?"

"Yes. Risa is usually quite concrete when it comes to things like that. I think she's indecisive because of Darren."

Two pairs of sharp and way too assessing blue eyes swung in her direction. Risa tried and failed to keep herself from blushing.

"It's not exactly easy to find a rental in the summer in Diamond Creek. Just about everywhere is booked all summer with tourists. I figured I could stay with Trey and Emma, and maybe Darren, until I have some time to look around."

Jack nodded slowly. "With it already September, I'd think you could find a place by now. As for Darren, what *is* the status with you and him?"

Risa sighed. Problem was, she was all over the place when it came to Darren. She couldn't stop thinking about him. When they were together, she all but singed herself on the passion that flared between them. The tiny corner of her heart that clung to silly ideas desperately wanted her to give love a chance, while the cynical side of her didn't know if it was worth the bother.

She fiddled with the stem of her wineglass. "I don't know what the status is. When we're together, things are…really good. But we don't talk about, you know…*us,* so I'm not sure what he wants. His sister is staying with him right now. She told me about an accident he responded to in Seattle when he was a cop there and said he hadn't really dated since then. She seems to think we're meant to be, but I'm not sure what I want, and I sure as hell don't know what he wants."

When she looked up, Jack and Ethan both looked concerned.

"Don't look at me like that. What are you two thinking?" she asked.

They started to speak at once. Ethan paused and gestured for Jack to continue.

"Maybe you should ask him," Jack said softly.

Risa closed her eyes and took a breath. Talking to Darren meant making herself vulnerable. Though she was mostly done with denying how much he meant to her, the idea of allowing him to see inside her heart was a trip-wire to her fears that she wasn't good enough for him. She wasn't even enough for a loser like Brad. Darren was so much more. To put her heart on the line and risk being rejected…she didn't know if she was ready to face that.

CHAPTER 17

"Aunt Risa!" Stuart squealed as he hurled himself against her legs.

"Hey Stu," Risa replied as she leaned over to greet him upside down, which never failed to elicit a giggle.

With a ruffle of his hair, her nephew gave her a smacking kiss on the cheek before he ran back outside. The fall wind blew the door wide.

"Stuart, don't forget the door," his mother called out.

The sound of running feet across the deck was muffled when the door swung shut quickly.

Emma shook her head before turning to pull Risa into a hug. "Hey there, you're finally here to stay," she said with a quick grin before stepping away and waving Risa into the living room.

Emma plunked on the couch beside baby Janet who was sound asleep in a detached car seat. Risa sat on the other side of Janet and leaned over to place a soft kiss on her forehead.

"Wow, she looks bigger every time I see her," Risa observed.

Emma chuckled. "I see her every day and it still blows my mind. She gets fussy if I take her out of her car seat once she's asleep, so I carry her around in it," Emma said with a shrug. "So, what's the plan now that you're here?"

Risa shrugged. "I'm here, and I have to figure out where I'm staying. I've been so busy getting organized between the gallery and packing that it seemed like I couldn't find the time to find a place to rent."

"You can stay with us as long as you need," Emma said with a warm smile.

Risa chuckled and shook her head. "I know you and Trey don't mind me staying with you. And I love visiting. But I need to find my own place now that I'll be living here. It's one thing to use your place as a crash pad for weekend, but that's not a good long-term plan."

Emma's eyes took on a sly gleam. "Seems like you have more than one place to use as a crash pad. Would that be why you're not sure if you're staying here tonight?"

Risa's face heated and she swore silently. Diamond Creek was a tight-knit community. It was a wonder Emma hadn't asked her about Darren sooner. Though Emma hadn't said his name, Risa knew without a doubt that Emma knew about him. She bit her lip and sighed. "Okay, what have you heard and what does Trey know?"

Emma giggled. "I heard you've been seeing Darren Thomas. His sister's been here for a bit and she's, um, chatty." Emma paused and threw an understanding smile her way. "I'm not trying to give you grief. I only said something because you might as well hear it from me that you've officially landed on the gossip radar in Diamond Creek. As far as I'm concerned, Darren is wonderful. For starters, he was a huge help with everything that happened with my ex, but he's also a solid good guy and pretty easy on the eyes. To be honest, I'm not sure what Trey knows. Believe it or not, I only heard something this morning when I stopped by Misty Mountain Café. Susie was there, and somehow she'd met Darren's sister—no one escapes Susie's notice. You'd think since she just had a baby, she'd be busy, but she's all over town as usual with little Patrick in a sling wherever she goes."

"So what did Susie hear from Hallie?" Risa asked.

"Susie's version is that Hallie is ecstatic and thinks you're amazing. Before you go worrying about what Trey thinks, he has nothing but good things to say about Darren, so if he had an opinion, he'd be happy for you. I haven't had a chance to ask him, but I'm thinking he hasn't heard anything. He'd have said something if he did. On a more serious note, Susie said something about what Darren went through and how it's so great he's finally seeing someone. Care to fill me in on your version?"

Risa chewed the inside of her cheek. Jack's gentle suggestion that she talk with Darren tumbled through her mind. Her version of what was going on between her and Darren was a jumble, seeing as she couldn't think straight about him. But Emma was a good listener, not to mention a therapist, and maybe it would help to talk.

Simply thinking about talking about it flushed her again. With a sigh, she brushed her bangs out of her eyes and glanced at Emma whose blue eyes were steady and calm.

"My version, huh? Okay, I'll try. I met Darren the day I drove through the guardrail. To be honest, there was chemistry right off the bat. I haven't been much for dating seriously because it usually blows up in my face, so I figured maybe we could have some fun and we'd go our merry ways. But it hasn't been so simple. I mean..." she paused, blushing furiously. "You have to promise me you're not going to tell Trey all of this. I forget you're my sister-in-law half the time because you're such a good friend, but I don't really want Trey to hear everything, if you know what I mean."

Emma grinned and crossed her heart. "I tell Trey a lot of things, but I definitely don't tell him the personal details of my friends' love lives even if it so happens to involve his sister."

Risa nodded. "I figured, but just making sure..." Another deep breath and she continued. "Things are, well, amazing with Darren when we're together. When I say amazing, I mean nothing else comes close. And, ugh..." She ran her hands through her hair and leaned her head back against the couch, staring at the ceiling. "I didn't expect to feel the way I do. Aside from the fact that he's seriously good in bed, he's...a really good guy. I like him. A lot more than I planned on. But the thing is, we don't talk about us like we're a couple. Like for instance, he doesn't talk about it, but he's had nightmares a few times when I've been there. Like the kind where he wakes up covered in sweat. I don't know what it means. Maybe he doesn't want to talk to me..."

Risa rolled her head to the side and glanced at Emma. She wasn't sure how much it was okay to tell her, not because Emma wouldn't keep it private but because it was Darren's story to tell. It worried her that his nightmares and the accident behind them interfered with him being open and intimate with her. She didn't know if it was because of him, or because he didn't want to be intimate with *her* specifically. She elected to keep it general. "Hallie told me about something he went through in Seattle when he was a cop there and said he hadn't dated anyone since then. That's why she's all excited about us."

Risa sat quietly for a moment after she finished speaking. One of the things she loved about Emma was she considered her responses before offering them. Janet shifted and gurgled between them. Risa lifted her head and leaned to check on her. Janet was still sound asleep, her tiny hands fisted under her chin. Her sweet innocence elicited a flash of longing for something Risa hadn't allowed herself to consider. Darren was the first and only man she'd been with whom she could imagine creating a family with. The thought took her breath away. She abruptly looked away from Janet, willing her mind to behave. She looked to Emma again.

"Well?" Now the quiet was making Risa impatient.

"Things are a bit farther down the road than I'd have guessed. Sounds to me that 'like' might not quite capture how you feel about Darren."

Risa's heart slammed against her ribs. Leave it to Emma to go right to the soft spot, the place Risa shied away from whenever her heart murmured loud enough she couldn't ignore it.

"What do you mean?"

Emma looked at her carefully. "I'm thinking about

how you talked about—who was that guy you were dating?"

"Brad." Risa rolled her eyes at the mere thought of him. "He turned out to be a complete jerk, by the way."

"Good to know you're not with him anymore then. Back to my point, when you talked about him, well, he sounded like a guy you liked. You were interested, but taking it slow. That kind of thing. But the way you talk about Darren, well, it sounds like something much deeper."

Risa's throat tightened and her heart kept bumping up against her ribs. Emma was plainly pointing out what had her so tied in knots. She put her face in her hands and groaned.

"You don't need to tell me this has thrown you off guard. I'd have guessed that on my own. This doesn't have to be a bad thing. Darren's a great guy," Emma said softly.

Risa lifted her head up again and looked at Emma. "I know he is. I just...I didn't expect this. I don't know what he wants. Hallie's all excited and it's cute and all, but I'm not so sure Darren feels the same way. I don't want to get my hopes up and have it blow up in my face."

Emma sighed. "Oh right. That part. I conveniently forgot about that. Sucks to want something so much you're afraid to reach out and grab it, huh?"

Risa nodded vigorously. "Yes! So what the hell do I do?"

"Not to state the obvious, but maybe you should talk to him. For all you know, he feels the same way and is nervous to talk about it."

Risa glared at Emma. "Are you sure you didn't talk to Jack or Ethan about this?"

Emma's shoulders shook with her laugh. "No! When would I do that?"

"I don't know, but they said the same thing last night. Like it's easy to tell someone you're way into them and you didn't mean for it to happen and hey how do they feel." She rolled her eyes.

Emma giggled before her eyes sobered. "I didn't say it would be easy. I just figure why sit here and stew over it. You have to start the ball rolling somehow."

"I know, I know."

* * *

DARREN STOOD by the coffee maker waiting for the coffee to be ready. His head whipped up when he heard his name.

Travis stepped into the room from the open door that led to the fire station. "Hey man, how's it going?" Travis clapped him on the shoulder before sprawling in a chair at the table in the break room.

Darren quickly poured a cup of coffee and joined Travis at the table. "Busy. How about you?" he asked as he dumped cream into his coffee and took a welcome sip.

Travis shrugged, shifting quickly to stand and pour his own cup of coffee. "Busy as hell. The worst of fire season's over, but that damn fire up north on the peninsula just won't quit. Too much beetle kill's made it ideal for fire. We've been called up almost every week for shifts. If you want some extra cash, sign on one of these weeks. I'll be damn glad when the snow flies."

Darren nodded. "Yeah, heard you guys have been taking turns up there. I might join you one of these weeks. Things are finally slowing down for me now that the tourists are blowing out of town along with the fall weather."

Sylvia walked by the break room door and backed up to enter. "I've been looking for you. Oh, hi Travis," she said, turning her warm smile on him. "I haven't seen you in weeks."

Travis stood from the table and stepped to Sylvia's side, dropping a kiss on her cheek. "Been too busy. How are you?"

Sylvia nodded. "Just fine, dear. You boys be careful when you go up north again."

"Always." Travis glanced to Darren. "Catch you later," he said with a wave before leaving.

Sylvia filled a cup of coffee and turned back to Darren. "You've got a stack of reports to sign off on. Do you want me to bring them to you now?"

Darren stood. "Might as well." He started to turn and leave when he felt Sylvia's hand on his arm.

"Need something else?" he asked.

"Just thought I'd mention I'm tickled to hear you're seeing someone."

Darren experienced a flash of irritation. He couldn't shake the vague uneasiness he felt about Risa, an uneasiness triggered entirely by the fact that he could hardly stop thinking about her. His desire to see her again pounded in rhythm with his heart. Even before the accident and his choice to steer clear of anything serious, he'd never been...obsessed with anyone like this. He knew she'd moved here yesterday and the ache to see her was visceral. He tried to keep his distance because he knew she intended for last night to be a family night, but he'd had to hold himself back from texting her to see if she'd stop by. It was getting ridiculous. Meanwhile, he had Hallie chirping about how excited she was. He couldn't get away from it, and now Sylvia. He managed a tight smile to which Sylvia arched a brow. She had enough sense to leave it alone, and he made his way to his office.

Later that afternoon, he called Travis and asked him to put him on the back up list for the next flight up for the Diamond Creek crew for the fire up north. He had the time and figured it might shake his brain off the broken record that was Risa. His mind had lost all discipline when it came to her. The wish for something more, something permanent, was pushing against the barriers he'd built around his heart.

CHAPTER 18

A few days later, Darren walked into Risa's new place after work. He was a tad saner than he'd been the last few weeks after Risa had stayed with him the night before last. He'd come to view her like a drug addiction. If he got a fix, his brain didn't spin in circles thinking about her constantly. Though he couldn't claim personal experience with drug addiction, he imagined it was like that. While he wasn't putting his health at risk, his heart was definitely on the line. But he thought maybe he had the key to handling the situation. Perhaps he'd gotten so worked up over her because he only saw her here and there when she was still in Anchorage. With her living here now, he could date her like a normal person and see her every few days without going bonkers in his mind.

He stepped over some boxes on the floor and glanced around. She'd rented a small apartment in downtown Diamond Creek. It was the upstairs of a house converted into a separate apartment. The kitchen and living room comprised an open area in front with a large picture window. Two bedrooms and a bathroom were off an alcove in the back. It was more than enough space for her. Hardwood floors, granite counters and updated stainless steel appliances brightened what could have been a utilitarian space. A small woodstove added a touch of charm and could easily heat the entire apartment.

The house sat on Main Street and overlooked a marshy field with the bay and mountains in the distance. The sky was cloudy with shafts of lavender and pink cutting through the clouds from the setting sun. A brisk wind stirred whitecaps on the bay. A stand of birch to the side of the field fluttered, yellow leaves blowing off in the fall wind. The fireweed's glorious burst of fuchsia had faded with blanched petals scattered on the ground. Bright red and orange leaves from the low bushes dotted the landscape. He glanced to the mountains, wondering when termination dust would fall—the first snow that coated the mountaintops and served as the harbinger of winter.

He followed rustling sounds and found Risa in one of the bedrooms surrounded by boxes. She glanced up and put her hands on her hips. Her hair was in a rumple around her face, dark strands falling across her eyes. She wore a pair of faded leggings that hugged her voluptuous hips, paired with a bright red t-shirt that managed to accentuate her breasts. He got hard just looking at her, and she wasn't even trying. In fact, she looked irritable and tired. She sat down on the bed with a thud.

"Now I remember why I never pushed too hard to move here. I've thought about it for years, but it's so much work. Good thing I'm here now because if I'd had this day before I got here, I'd have changed my mind." She stretched her arms behind her back and glanced over at him.

"How was your day?"

Darren tried not to stare at her breasts, but she'd clasped her hands behind her back, which pushed them forward. He forced his eyes up to her face while his pulse galloped and lust thrummed through him. "Pretty good. This time of year is nice because things slow down at the station without so many tourists around. Do you want some help unpacking?" he asked, thinking something to do would help him get his body under control.

Risa let her arms fall and pushed herself up from the bed. "If you're offering, I'll take any help you want to give."

Darren tugged his jacket off and tossed it on a chair by the window. "Tell me what you want to go where."

An hour later, he discovered he and Risa worked quite well together. She wasn't fussy or picky about anything and preferred efficiency. She'd given him rough guidance on which boxes went where and was happy to have him unpack however he saw fit. They'd gotten the kitchen almost completely organized and were now working in what would be Risa's bedroom. He was relieved to be focused on something as he'd gotten his mind off of how good it would feel to run his hands over the curves hiding underneath her leggings and t-shirt. She'd given him free rein to simply open boxes and told him to ask if he wasn't sure where something could go.

He reached the bottom box in a stack. The label read 'Bathroom/bedroom.' With a flick of his pocketknife, the tape split and he opened the box. The top was occupied with obvious bathroom items, such as shampoo. After carting those items into the bathroom, he discovered a towel layered over the bottom portion of the box. By this point, he was on autopilot and simply tugged the towel out of the way. The control he'd congratulated himself on a few minutes ago evaporated. He was staring at what appeared to be her personal toy collection. At a glance, his eyes took in a bright purple vibrator snug beside a pink one with some kind of special attachment. His brain instantly conjured a picture of Risa using one of these. Just like that, his body was hijacked again. His cock was rock hard. He didn't realize he'd groaned aloud until Risa walked into the room.

"Everything okay? You have no idea how much help you've been. The kitchen's done, the living room's almost unpacked and I bet we'll finish these boxes in just a few minutes," she said, cheerfully oblivious to his current state.

Darren's head whipped up. She stood at the foot of the bed, her cheeks flushed, and a streak of dirt on her arm. A curious look flashed through her eyes when she met his. She stepped to his side and looked into the box.

"Oh," she said. The word fell with a soft breath.

She glanced up at him, her pulse beating visibly in her neck. He tried to rein himself in, but what little control he had was shattered when he saw the answering desire in her eyes. Moving swiftly, he tugged her against him. Her head tilted back, her mouth opening under his instantly. He kissed her as if he was drowning, and she was the air he needed to survive.

Without breaking his lips from hers, he wrapped an arm around her waist and turned to sit on the bed, using his other arm to shove everything out of the way in one quick swipe. Risa didn't hold back, which he loved about her. She pushed him back against the bed, straddling him and circling her hips against his cock. He was so hard, he could barely stand it and groaned against her mouth. He pushed her up and tore her shirt off, reaching around her back to unhook her bra. He paused for a long moment and just looked at her. Her breasts swayed in front of him, her nipples peaked. He reached up to roll them between his thumbs and forefingers.

Her breath came in fitful gasps. Leaning up, he tugged one nipple into his mouth and sucked deeply. She bucked against him, crying out. He did the same to her other nipple. Her eyes were dark and wild when he paused to glance up at her. She pushed back swiftly and stood, tearing at his jeans. In seconds, they were skin to skin, their limbs tangling on the bed as they rolled against each other.

Darren pulled Risa's wrists above her head, holding them in place with one hand. He paused to look at her. Her breasts rose and fell with her ragged breath. Her nipples glistened from his mouth. Keeping his eyes on hers, he dragged his free hand down her abdomen, savoring the soft curve. Her mouth opened on a gasp when he slid his fingers through her dark curls and dipped into her folds. She was dripping wet, he almost came at the feel of how turned on she was. He'd meant to tease her and then sink into her, but he needed more. Releasing her wrists, he shifted down her body, dusting kisses along the way. He shouldered her legs apart and brought his mouth against her. The salty tang of her desire consumed him. He stroked his tongue through her folds, circling her clit and following the rhythm of her hips, which shifted and bucked under his mouth.

"Darren...I need..."

"This?" he questioned as he slid two fingers into her channel, stroking deeply in and out, just as he sucked on her clit. She convulsed around him, her cries broken by her gasps for air. He stilled his fingers and slowly brought his mouth away. In a quick move, he shifted on top of her, his elbows bracketing her face. He surged smoothly and completely into her. Her name fell from his lips in a groan. Her channel pulsed around him, hugging him in its tight, wet grip. He held still for a moment and met her eyes. The bare intimacy of the moment slammed into his chest. Her eyes widened and vulnerability arced in their dark depths. He cupped her cheek and brought his lips to hers as he began to slowly stroke into her.

He forced himself to give her time to peak again, holding back until she was gasping his name. When he felt her begin to convulse around his length, he let go, coming in a shout against her. He shifted slightly to keep his weight from crushing her. They lay still, a tangle of sweaty limbs and broken breathing. He brushed a loose lock of hair away from her eyes. He felt so close to her, it startled him. He didn't know what to make of it, so he simply held still inside. When she turned her head and met his eyes with a hint of a smile, he relaxed a little.

"So, uh, that box of yours..."

* * *

DARREN KICKED the door closed behind him with his booted foot and strode quickly to the kitchen counter to dump an armful grocery bags. Hallie breezed in the room and immediately came over to start putting groceries away.

"Hey! How was your day?" she asked cheerfully.

"The usual."

"Does the usual include a date with Risa tonight?"

Darren paused and glanced at Hallie. She grinned and continued putting groceries away. He elected to ignore her question.

After a few moments of silence between them, Hallie closed the refrigerator and leaned on it after she placed the last item inside. She crossed her arms over her chest and glared at him. If he weren't so on edge about Risa, he might have laughed. Hallie attempting to look angry was rare and verged on comical. Her brown hair was in a ponytail on the top of her head. She wore her glasses today, the frames bright blue and round. The blue matched the t-shirt she wore. Hallie was generally a cheery sort, so any annoyance from her was uncommon.

"What?" he asked.

"What's wrong with asking you about seeing Risa? She lives in Diamond Creek now. You've seen her pretty often the last few weeks since she moved here. I'm excited for you, and she's awesome."

Hallie blithely zeroed in on what made him shift uncomfortably where he stood as he wondered how to get a handle on this. Way back when he met Risa and she nearly blew his mind with a kiss, he tried to slow things down because he didn't want to treat her like some casual fling. But he'd had some crazy idea he could remain rational and in control. With Risa, he was anything but. He drove by her apartment repeatedly every day—not because he purposefully did so, but because she lived smack in the middle of town and being a cop involved plenty of driving around town. An unintended side effect of the mind-blowing sex they had was that every time he happened to drive by, his mind revisited another moment with her, the result being he was in a semi-constant state of arousal.

Meanwhile, he had Hallie constantly dropping hints, Sylvia making feeble attempts to tactfully ask about Risa, and his own conflicted feelings. He thought back to Jared's quick observation that he should avoid overthinking. Much easier said than done. At the sound of an aggrieved sigh coming from Hallie, he realized he hadn't replied to her. Because...overthinking.

"Hallie, don't get me wrong, Risa *is* awesome. I know you're excited about us, but give me a little time here. I'm not so sure I'm ready to dive in the deep end yet. I don't know if she is either."

Hallie let her arms fall and sighed. "I figured you'd say something like that."

She looked so disappointed, he felt compelled to explain. "We haven't even known each other that long..."

Hallie pushed away from the refrigerator, cutting him off with a wave. "Darren, I was just excited for you. That's all. But don't be stupid and stand in your own way for something amazing," she said as she walked off.

Darren leaned against the counter with a sigh. He wished he could get everyone off his back long enough to let him think for himself. Maybe he was standing in his own way. He didn't question that Risa was amazing. He questioned his ability to be whole enough to open himself up to someone else. Though he was in so deep with Risa, he'd lost control of the situation and had let her much farther inside his heart than he'd ever intended.

CHAPTER 19

*R*isa let herself into the gallery and immediately got to work. She'd arranged for the newly painted sign for Midnight Sun Arts to be hung today. Within moments, two men showed up with the sign and got to work. The inside of the gallery was almost ready to go. Ethan and Jack were headed down to Diamond Creek today. Once the sign was up, and they gave the go ahead, they'd open the gallery later this week. She'd hemmed and hawed over whether it was a good idea to open on the tail end of tourist season, but Ethan and Jack thought the holiday sales would get them on good footing. They also insisted they didn't want to wait through the winter and attempt to open when the hordes of tourists descended in the spring.

As she checked and rechecked the displays and reviewed inventory, her mind kept rubbing thoughts of Darren around. She alternated between pulse pounding fantasies about the next time she saw him and wondering what the hell she'd gotten herself into.

Her heart was treading on dangerous ground. She had moments when she wanted to try to talk to him about what she was to him and where they were going, if anywhere, but she found herself holding back. When they were tangled up in each other, so close she couldn't tell her heartbeat from his, she thought perhaps he felt as she did. But outside of that, Darren's reserve held. She pondered what Hallie told her, but didn't dare ask him about it.

The door to the gallery swung open, and Ethan and Jack entered.

Ethan paused in the center of the room and spun in a circle, while Jack walked to her side behind the counter and gave her a quick kiss.

"It looks perfect," Jack said softly.

Ethan came to a stop and held his arms wide. "I love it! You've done wonders in the last few weeks. Precisely why we wanted you to manage it. We haven't even had to worry."

He strode to her side and tugged her into a quick hug before leaning against the counter. Jack had already started perusing through the gallery email on the computer.

Ethan eyed her. "So have you talked to Darren yet?"

"More than once actually," she deadpanned.

Jack chuckled, but didn't look up.

Ethan rolled his eyes. "Let me clarify. I meant have you *talked* to him?"

Risa couldn't fight the flush that rose up her neck and face. She shook her head quickly.

Ethan eyed her for a long moment. She felt like a coward. Not because of Ethan asking her about it, but because she shouldn't be so damn scared to try to talk to Darren. That's what reasonable adults did. But she was half-afraid of his answer and what it might mean for her heart. She'd thought herself recovered from the embarrassment of one of her closest friends basically stealing her boyfriend right under her nose. And perhaps she had in some ways. But her heart was feeling a bit too exposed with Darren. He was too much of everything she wanted.

Jack turned away from the computer and glanced between her and Ethan, his eyes pausing on Ethan. "Cut her some slack. Risa gets to figure this out in her own time and her own way."

Ethan's mouth dropped in mock outrage as he reached over and cuffed Jack on the shoulder. "She's had weeks already! I bet she's been getting plenty of action between the sheets."

Risa couldn't hold back her laugh. "So what if I have?"

Jack shook his head, his eyes concerned. While he wouldn't be as bossy as Ethan, she knew he'd worry about her. She wished she could tell him not to bother, but she was worried about herself.

Her laugh faded. "I know I need to talk to him. I'm afraid I'm in too deep already," she said with a sigh.

* * *

HOURS LATER, Risa walked along the beach. She'd had a wonderful dinner with Jack and Ethan at The Boathouse Café. After they'd driven away, she'd followed a path from the parking lot onto the beach. Fall wind gusted off the bay. The long summer days were rapidly shortening. The sun was setting in a burst of soft colors—pink, gold, and lavender swirling through the sky. A raft of sea otters floated within view of the shore. She counted eighteen of them clustered together, drifting on their backs in the water. Their furred faces turned her direction when she walked by, and she couldn't help but smile. Two otters rolled onto their sides and dove under the water, coming up in front of the raft of their companions. They watched her curiously and then rolled onto their backs again, rising and falling in the soft roll of waves.

A bright red lava rock caught her eyes, and she tucked it in her pocket. Her fleece jacket didn't do much to keep the wind out, so she eventually turned back and drove home, chilled through. When she pulled up at her apartment, her phone beeped. Glancing down, she saw a text from Darren.

Okay if I stop by?

She forced herself to wait, letting herself into her apartment, kicking off her shoes and hanging her jacket before she pulled her phone out again.

Of course! When will you be over?

The thing was, she couldn't say no. It was him. She jumped at any chance to see him. Her heart did a little happy dance. Her body thrummed with anticipation. She knew she had to talk to him soon, but she wasn't going to let that interfere with seeing him tonight. Just as she began to wonder why he hadn't replied, she heard footsteps on the stairs outside leading to her apartment. A quick knock, and she flung the door open. Darren stood there, his chocolate gaze on her instantly, his cheeks ruddy from the cold. His jacket hung loosely from his broad shoulders, his muscled chest outlined against the thin cotton of his t-shirt.

Risa grabbed his hand and tugged him against her. "Hi," she said, her voice husky.

The corner of his mouth kicked up in a smile, and his eyes darkened. "Hi, how…"

She cut him off with a kiss, slipping her hand around his neck and yanking his mouth to hers. Darren didn't hesitate and instantly swept his tongue inside her mouth, stroking against hers. Kissing him was so decadent, she could have done it all day. He never rushed through it and treated kisses as important as the main act. Actually, he treated every moment when his hands were on her like that. Slow, sensual attention to detail that left her gasping and stole her senses.

Desire filtered around them, sensation teeming in her center and swirling outward. Darren stepped closer, his hard body coming against hers. He kicked the door shut behind him, a rush of chilled air whooshing through the room when he did. Her skin pebbled and he pulled back, sliding his hands up and down her arms.

"You're cold," he said.

"I'm okay."

He glanced around. "It's freezing in here. Have you turned on your heat yet?"

When she shook her head, he stepped away and walked to the woodstove. He quickly grabbed firewood from the small rack beside the stove and got a fire started. Warmth immediately began to circulate in the air. The sight of the flames through the small window in the woodstove door made her feel warmer. He stood and walked to the door, hanging his jacket up and toeing his boots off before turning to step to her side.

He paused in front of her, his heated gaze focused on her. He tucked a loose lock of hair behind her ear, shivers chasing in the wake of his brief touch.

"Now...where were we?" he asked, his voice low and taut.

Heat pooled in her belly. He stepped closer until his body was against hers. Arousal spiked through her as he leaned down and brought his mouth to hers, brushing his lips back and forth. His hands slipped up her sides to cup her breasts. Her nipples tightened under his touch. This kiss was slow, deep and devouring. His hands shifted away from her breasts, and they instantly ached for his touch again. One of his hands set to work unbuttoning her blouse while the other roamed around her back, sliding up in a sure stroke and down to cup her bottom and press her hips to his. The feel of his hard, hot length against her cleft brought a whimper from her throat. Lust curled through her, unwinding in a wave, her whole body keening for more.

He slowly pulled back, tugging her bottom lip with his teeth. A tiny voice in a distant corner of her mind tried to raise the alarm—this was too much, too intense, she was in too deep. She batted it away and surrendered to the depth of want she felt. He began walking them toward the couch. One of his thighs slid in and out between hers with each step, brushing across the nub of her desire, teasing her to the point of madness. Her blouse fell open when her knees bumped the couch. In one smooth motion, he spun them around, seating himself on the couch in front of her, his eyes level with her breasts. He tugged her blouse off, her bra following.

His hands cupped her breasts, rolling her nipples

between his fingers as he glanced up at her through his dark lashes. The only word she could form came out.

"Please..."

Darren gave her what she wanted and brought his warm, wet mouth to one breast, laving it, tugging it between his teeth and then turning to the other. When he pulled back, her nipples were so taut it verged on painful. They glistened, dusky pink, in the flickering light from the woodstove. His eyes pinned to hers, he unbuttoned her jeans and slowly tugged them down her hips, his hands caressing her as he dragged them down her legs. She kicked them out of the way and stood before him in nothing but the scrap of black silk she wore.

He was silent for a long moment before a soft groan came from his throat. She felt bare and exposed and unable to turn away from the heat of his gaze. He slipped a hand between her legs, caressing the damp silk. She gasped at the feel of his fingers stroking lightly back and forth across the wet evidence of her desire. He cupped her bottom and tugged her closer until his mouth was inches from her. In a quick move, he hooked a finger on the edge of her panties, yanking them down until they fell around her ankles. Anticipation buzzed through her veins. Feverish with want, she waited, her core throbbing with need. In slow motion, he now stroked into her folds, drenched with desire. A broken sob came from her throat. His thumb grazed her clit, circling in her moisture, before he brought his mouth to her.

She cried out, her hips bucking against him. He held her in place, one hand cupping her bottom, the other stroking into and out of her channel. His mouth teased her beyond desperation. Wet, heated strokes of his tongue, his fingers plunging in and out. She tumbled into the hot rush. Her orgasm spiraled through her, his name falling from her lips again and again and again. Had he not been holding her in his hands, she'd have collapsed. He gradually stilled his mouth and fingers and pulled away.

Giving her no time to gather her scattered senses, he brought his lips to her breasts again, teasing them with kisses and nips, his warm hands skating over her body, cupping her soft curves. In moments, she was teetering on the edge of wild desire again. He stood abruptly and turned to move behind her. She fell to her knees on the couch, almost collapsing completely before she managed to rest her elbows on the back of the couch. She heard the rustle of clothes being torn off and falling to the floor. She knew the moment he turned and saw her. He growled, her name following in a ragged gasp.

She was so desperate for him to fill her, she arched her back, tilting her hips up. She felt the brush of his cock against her hips, the velvety skin hot and hard, and a slow glide into her slick heat. He drove into her to the hilt. She sighed in relief as he stretched her aching channel. He held still for a long moment. When he spoke, his voice was slurred.

"Risa...what you do to me..."

In answer, she shifted her hips, drawing forward. He chased her motion and began to surge in and out. He curled a hand around her hips, his fingers gripping her soft flesh. His other palm slid up her spine, strong and sure, coming to rest on her shoulder and he pounded into her, pulling her against him, each stroke driving all the way in. Shudders began to wrack her body, pressure gathering with each stroke until her climax stormed through her, her body arching with her scream. He pulled out and surged back in deeply, her name following in a guttural cry. Her head fell forward, his hand relaxed on her shoulder and slid down to rest in the center of her back. A tear slid down her cheek, she was so overcome.

They remained like that for several quiet moments, the fire crackling and their broken breaths slowing. Darren finally pulled out of her and curled an arm under her hips. He lifted her into his arms. She couldn't bear to look at him. The intimacy was too much. She was relieved that he didn't talk, but simply shifted her weight to hold her firmly as he carried her to her bedroom.

CHAPTER 20

*D*arren stood by his office window and looked out over Kachemak Bay. The sky was slate gray, the water tossed by the wind. Termination dust coated the mountains after the first snow had fallen during the night. He'd left Risa's place this morning and been half out of his mind since then. He could hardly bear to be away from her and was terrified he was losing control of the situation.

He'd woken with another nightmare last night. As she had before, she woke with him and quietly waited while he showered. When he returned to bed, she'd proceeded to drive him out of his mind with sultry kisses and a mind-altering blowjob. Again, he fell asleep, the machinations of his haunted dreams a distant memory. She still hadn't said anything to him about his nightmares, and he wondered if Hallie had told her anything. He'd never asked her to keep it a secret, but he wasn't so sure how he felt if Risa knew what had happened. He didn't like the feeling that she might know he was something other than strong. He was already feeling too close for comfort, too vulnerable with her. Last night before he'd gone over, he'd promised himself he wasn't going to see her. He'd sought to find a way to bring the situation back under control. He'd wanted to prove to himself he could resist the urge to see her. He'd planned to have a quiet night at home watching whatever sports he could find to hold his interest. Hallie had been out with a friend, so he'd had the house to himself.

His commitment to this plan was much weaker than he'd thought. He'd given in and texted her right after he had a solitary dinner. Waking up with her was a heaven he couldn't have imagined. She was a cuddler and tangled her legs with his, mashing her lush curves against him. It was a damn miracle he managed to even get out of bed. So he'd almost run out the door in his haste to get control of himself. She was busy enough getting ready for her workday that if she noticed, she let it slide. He'd offered the excuse that he had an early meeting—a flat out lie.

He turned away from the window and strode out of his office and through the break room to the fire station. He found Travis standing with some of the crew in the fire chief's office.

"Hey, when are you guys slated to head up north for the next shift on that fire?" Darren asked.

Travis grinned. "Funny you ask. We're on the schedule to leave tomorrow. They're using back up whenever they can get it. Want to sign on?"

"I'm in. What time are we leaving?" Darren asked quickly.

"We drive up at five in the morning," Travis replied.

"See you then," Daren said, turning and heading back to his office.

He needed to break this pattern with Risa. He needed to get his feelings under control. Though he couldn't imagine life without Risa anymore, he was frantic to rein himself in. Being out of town for a few days might do the trick. It would also get his brain back under control. He wouldn't be able to focus on anything other than the fire.

* * *

DARREN WATCHED as the landscape rolled by underneath the helicopter he rode in alongside six other firefighters from the Diamond Creek crew. They'd driven to Kenai this morning and had immediately been shuttled over to a helicopter. The fire in question was north of Diamond Creek on the outskirts of the Kenai National Wildlife Refuge near a remote area lightly populated with homes. Crews had been rotating in and out for weeks trying to contain the quickly moving fire. Much of Alaska's spruce forests had become tinderboxes in the aftermath of the scourge of spruce bark beetle, a non-native beetle that had made its way to Alaska from Asia and devastated massive swathes of once healthy spruce forests. There were miles upon miles of dead spruce trees, easy and quick to burn. As a result, forest fires were more dangerous and spread rapidly.

Travis was seated beside Darren. "Damn, it's not looking good," he said, gesturing ahead.

Darren looked in the direction Travis pointed. Smoke lay in a haze for miles. Blackened sections of forest began to appear. A few other helicopters were visible in the distance. Some flew over with fire retardant and water, while others carried firefighters. Darren enjoyed not having to be the leader when he did back up with the crew. All he had to do was follow orders. Their helicopter landed, and he was sent out with two others to try to hold a line that had been established. The fire was teasing its way too close to some small communities and if left unchecked, it would torch them within days. Alaskans were practical souls and many had already evacuated, some helping to fight the fire, others waiting it out away from the danger zones.

Darren tugged his heavy gear on and followed behind Travis and James, the two he'd been assigned to stay with. All around, smoke lay in a heavy blanket. The blackened trees rose in ghostly clusters as far as the eye could see. When they reached the area they were assigned to, they could see a green line of forest ahead—the area the fire hadn't crossed yet. The fall wind gusted, blowing smoke in his face. Risa passed through his mind. He missed her, her flashing dark eyes and her smile. More than anything, he missed the way he felt when he was with her—comfortable, yet teetering on the edge of that delicious wildness between them. He swore to himself and kept walking.

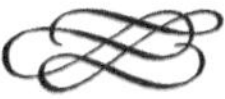

"When will he be back?" Risa asked Hallie.

She'd woken this morning to find a message from Darren that he was headed out to respond to a fire north of Diamond Creek. She'd known he did back up sometimes for the Diamond Creek crew, but she had somehow thought this was an on-paper kind of thing that meant he didn't actually fight fires. Her throat was tight and her stomach in knots over the thought that he would be out in the middle of the forest fire that had been raging for weeks. She didn't like it *at all.*

Hallie stood in front of Risa at the gallery. "He said it would be at least three days, maybe more."

Hallie had stopped by the gallery to take a look around. Her hazel eyes were apologetic and worried. She fiddled with the ponytail on her head, eventually tugging out the scarf that held it up, her hair falling in soft waves to her shoulders.

Risa felt a heavy weight in her stomach. She'd tried

calling Darren back, but he hadn't answered. She was angry and frightened at once. *Don't make a thing out of this. The Diamond Creek crew has been covering shifts on this fire for weeks now, and they've all come back just fine. Darren will too. That's not what you're afraid of.* Her mind taunted her. She didn't like it, but if she allowed herself to be honest, she was afraid of how much he'd come to mean to her. And this one action—leaving abruptly and not answering her calls—reinforced what she'd feared. That he didn't want something serious with her. He found a convenient way to create some space and used it.

Risa met Hallie's eyes. "Did he mention this before, or was this a last minute thing?"

Seriously, you're grilling her. Stop it.

Hallie chewed her lip and shrugged. "He didn't mention it, but then he doesn't always keep me in the loop. He's still getting used to me being around all the time. I'm sure he'd have told you sooner if he knew."

Risa came around the counter and walked to one of the displays, pointlessly adjusting a painting on the wall and rearranging a display of pottery. With a sigh, she turned back to Hallie. "I don't know if he would. If it seems like I'm mad, it's not with him. I think a little space might be good for us."

Hallie looked back at her, tapping her foot on the floor. "You know, I'm just going to say it. Darren is all messed up over you, and I think it's because he's scared of how much you mean to him," she said bluntly, her words tumbling out rapidly.

Risa's heart stuttered and then soared, hope unfurling inside. She batted it back. Just because his little sister thought she meant a lot to Darren didn't make it true. She took a slow breath, trying to calm her heart and get her romantic fever dreams under control.

"What makes you think that?"

Hallie's arms fell and she leaned against the display counter. "I may not be around much, but Darren and I have always been close. He doesn't show much, but he cares about people a lot. Even before the accident, he was kind of the strong, silent type, you know what I mean?"

At Risa's slow nod, Hallie continued. "And when that little boy and his parents died, Darren just closed down. I mean, he was still nice because he's always nice, but he stopped even dating. He never said it out loud, but I think he was freaking out because of those dumb nightmares—as if someone would think he was weak or something—and he didn't want anyone to see him like that. He's been a workaholic too. But since he's met you, he's happier than I've seen him in years since even before the accident. So yeah, if you're asking, I think he loves you and he's about going crazy because of it."

Risa's mind whirred and her heart leapt to her throat. Hallie had gone and spoken aloud what Risa would give anything to believe. To hear that Darren was happier since he'd met her sent a rush of hope through her. She stared at Hallie so long, Hallie waved at her. "Hello? Still with me?"

Risa shook her head sharply. Her heart still pounded and that damn hope was galloping through her. "I'm with you. I don't know you that well, but since we're talking…I don't know what the hell to do. Darren's not the only one who has, I don't know, issues with intimacy. I've got my own baggage, and I sure as hell didn't plan to fall for him like I have. So, if you're hypothesis is right…"

Hallie cut her off. "It's right. I know Darren."

Risa gave her a pointed look. "If you're right, what do you suggest I do about it? Whenever he gets back here."

Hallie chewed her lip again. "I don't think you're going to like this advice because I sure wouldn't, but you might have to show your cards first. He's so freaked out, if he has any concern that you don't feel the way he does, he's going to stick with the strong, silent routine. He's got that down, so it's his default mode. You're going to have to shake him out of it."

Risa's heart hammered against her ribs. What Hallie was suggesting meant putting herself out there, *way* out there, with a man who meant more to her than anyone ever had. She thought she'd been crushed by what happened with Brad. If she laid her heart on the line with Darren and he walked away, she'd be devastated.

Risa met Hallie's eyes. "All I can say is I'll take that on advisement."

Hallie's face fell. "Look, I know what I suggested would be scary. I'd be terrified and worried I was going to embarrass the hell out of myself. But I think it will work with him because he loves you. And he has a heart of gold. He won't be able to ignore his feelings for you if he knows you feel the same way. Please just give him a chance. I haven't seen him like this about anyone. You mean so much to him."

Risa couldn't help but feel Hallie's plea. She so clearly loved her brother and wanted the best for him. Risa just didn't know if she had it in her to fling her feelings out there—unprotected and exposed—and wait to see how Darren responded.

* * *

THE HEAT from the fire was fierce, compounded by the heavy gear and breathing apparatus he had to wear. Darren, Travis and James were methodically clearing brush near the fire line in an attempt to widen the line of protection. The thwack of helicopter blades, near and far, was constant. Just ahead of the direction they were moving, a helicopter flew low and sprayed fire retardant. A few homes were visible nearby. He prayed the residents had evacuated because they were in the line of fire now.

Darren's plan for this foray to get his mind off of Risa was turning out to be a spectacular failure. Even when he was deep in the middle of the fire, surrounded for miles by blackened forest with flames and smoke a constant presence, she sauntered through his thoughts—as if she owned them. He felt like a coward for not talking to her about leaving for a few days, but it had been an impulsive decision. When she hadn't answered when he called, he decided it was best that way and left a brief message. Now, he wondered if he'd managed to make himself look like he didn't care.

He kept moving, sweat dripping inside his gear. As they approached one of the nearby homes to establish a perimeter around it, he heard a shout and looked up.

Travis gestured to the home. Darren glanced to the home and saw a woman and two children watching them from the window. He looked behind the house to see the dead, dry spruce trees up in flames. The dirt road that led to the home cut through the area where the fire had travelled. The only reason Darren could guess the family stayed was that by the time they elected to leave, the fire blocked their only exit route.

He swore to himself and ran to catch up to Travis, James right behind him.

"We need to radio for one of the helicopters to circle back and try to douse those trees," Travis said, his voice muffled by his respirator.

James tugged his radio out and called in. He gave a quick shake of his head. "They flew back to refuel. It'll be another half hour before they can get back here."

Darren glanced around and swore. Without another word between them, they separated and moved toward the house to knock down the nearby trees and flammable tinder. The best they could hope for was to keep the fire far enough away to save the house.

Darren ran on adrenaline for the next half hour. Finally, Risa was out of his thoughts, but now, he'd have given anything to be thinking about her instead of working frantically to keep the fire away from the house. He conferred briefly with Travis and James at one point to identify the best direction to move with the mother and her children if it looked like they couldn't hold the line around the house. A wide stream ran through the area a short distance away. If all else failed, they'd head there and wait in the water if necessary.

Moments later, it was obvious they had to get the family out and move. The wind shifted, pushing the fire toward the house and them. The dry spruce crackled, a few trees toppling quickly in the wind and flames. Darren didn't have time to think as they pounded on the door. A little girl who stood no taller than his hip opened the door, her brown eyes wide. Impatience flared when he realized the family wasn't ready to leave. With Travis and James shouting for them to follow immediately, the little girl stood frozen by the door. She met Darren's eyes and pointed to a room to the side. He followed her point to find the mother frantically trying to lift an elderly woman out of a bed. The woman was asleep, her body frail.

Darren didn't stop to think. He strode over and lifted the elderly woman out of the mother's arms, setting her back in the bed. A wheelchair sat in the corner. He calculated he could run with the woman in the chair, perhaps safer for her than being lugged in his arms. Not to mention the condition she appeared to be in, she'd need somewhere to rest while they waited for the helicopter to return and airlift them out. He hollered through his mask for the mother and her two children to follow Travis and James. When the mother hesitated, both children clung to her. He swore and grabbed the wheelchair. He was as gentle as he could be as he moved the woman into the wheelchair. Her body was so frail, he worried he'd hurt her by moving her. Her eyes never opened. When he reached the door, he saw James at the front of the mother and one of the children, leading the way toward the stream with Travis holding back, attempting to persuade the little girl who'd answered the door to come with him. She was clinging to the railing at the foot of the stairs, refusing to budge.

Darren couldn't hear much with the wind, the fire

and his helmet and respirator mask muting every-thing. The dead trees, ideal fire fuel, continued to topple as the flames licked around them. He hollered Travis' name. When Travis lifted his head, the little girl turned to follow his gaze. As soon as she saw Darren with the woman he presumed to be her grandmother, she ran to his side. He couldn't take it if something happened to her because she waited. As soon as she reached his side, he grabbed her hand firmly. With Travis helping, they maneuvered the chair down a ramp adjacent to the stairs and rolled it quickly across the field to the side of the house. In the midst of this, Darren had to release the little girl's hand. Halfway across the field, he realized she wasn't following anymore and turned back.

She stood by the end of the ramp. As he turned to go back for her, horror welled inside when she ran up the ramp and back into the house. Wind gusted, sending flames spiraling against the bright blue sky. Darren wished he could move faster in his gear. His heart was in his throat. That split second when he reached for the little boy all those years ago flashed through his mind. He forced his mind back to now. Fire was dancing in the trees, skirting far too close to the house. He barreled through the door and saw the little girl curled up under the bed where the grand-mother had been, her knees tucked to her chest and her face buried against them—as if she could hide from the fire and find safety there.

He heard shouts and knew he had to move fast. The heat of the fire gusted through the open door. The crackle of burning trees was all around. He ran the short distance into the bedroom and reached for the little girl. Though tiny, her strength was surprising. She resisted his tug on her arm. Her body shook though not a sound came from her. Darren's pulse was pounding. Fear choked him. He wouldn't leave her behind. He knelt down, reached under the edge of the bed and dragged her out, lifting her fully into his arms. She was a tight ball and didn't make a sound. He moved as fast as he could, shouldering through the door and back outside, a wall of heat slamming him in the face.

The little girl began crying, her sobs strident through the cacophony of sounds echoing in his helmet. He knew from his work as a police officer and a firefighter that reason rarely drove responses when emotions were high. She began kicking against his legs, screaming and pointing at the house behind them. They were about halfway to the stream. Darren glanced ahead to see James had grabbed the hands of the mother and her other child and was tugging them along. The mother's neck was craned back, her eyes on them as they moved toward the stream.

The wind gusted, toppling trees into each other, one falling and bouncing on the roof of the house. Darren gestured for Travis to keep going. Darren began to run in Travis' wake while the little girl kicked at his legs. He kept moving, the crackle and hiss of burning trees behind them too close for comfort. His heart pounded frantically, his throat was tight, and flashes from his familiar nightmare flickered in his mind.

They finally reached the stream, ushering the family into the water and to the far side. James and Travis jointly lifted the wheelchair holding the elderly woman and set it on the sloping bank on the other side. Darren forced himself to breathe slowly, a task made far more difficult by the heat inside his helmet and respirator mask. He shoved his memories away and tried to focus on the moment. They sat in a small group beside the stream and watched the house go up in flames. The little girl now wouldn't let go of him. She stuck to his side like a burr.

He eventually got her to settle beside her mother. The fire blew through the house quickly, marching along the line of forest. The stream had been a good point to wait with the fire following the trees further down before jumping the stream a good half-mile below them in the field. Darren needed to get his nerves under control and his runaway memories in check. He kept telling himself this wasn't the accident, that the situation was as safe as possible right now. Though safe was relative considering they were surrounded by burned forest with the wind driving the fire forward. The saving grace was the section of the stream where they waited was clear of trees for a good distance in both directions. He glanced to the little girl, his throat tightening as he watched her climb into her mother's lap. The elderly woman in the wheelchair opened her eyes and looked toward the flames—so beautiful and destructive at once. Her eyes were filled with wonder, as if she was in awe of the force of the fire. She seemed unperturbed to have woken in her wheelchair by the stream, surrounded by her family and three strange firefighters.

Darren closed his eyes, fear pounding through his heart. *Stop thinking about that damn accident. It's been five years. That was then, this is now. Everyone got out okay.* It didn't work. His mind clung to the tiny slice of memory, playing it on a loop in his brain—the moment when he reached for that little boy. Sweat dripped on his skin inside his gear. James tore his respirator off and splashed water on his face. When Travis quickly followed suit, Darren did the same. The cold water was a balm and helped ease the tight feeling in his chest. As they waited and his mind kept disobeying his orders to stay focused, he found the only thing that kept him from mentally spiraling inside was to think of Risa. Her warm, dark eyes and full mouth, her throaty laugh and the feel of her body beside his.

He chuckled to himself when he realized he'd flipped the script in his head. He'd come to the backcountry to chase a fire to try to shake the grip Risa seemed to have on his heart, his body and his mind. And yet, when the demons of a single memory, a split second in time, came back to haunt him, he sought her out in his mind. For now, he let it be. With another splash of water on his face, relief washed through him. In the distance, he saw a helicopter crest the horizon. Moments later, the thwack of its rotating blades was a welcome sound.

He stood by with Travis and James as the helicopter slowly came down for a landing in the burned field. Time passed in a blur as they helped everyone get loaded into the helicopter. He would wait with Travis and James for another helicopter to carry them out since there wasn't room for all of them.

Hours passed as they waited, watching the fire move. The wind changed direction more than once. The sun began to set over the mountains. Streaks of red, orange and gold smudged in the haze of smoke hanging over the sky.

CHAPTER 22

*R*isa threaded her way through the gallery on its opening evening. They'd timed it to open on the date of a monthly arts event, First Friday, a common event in many communities. Art galleries stayed open late with refreshments, sales and special exhibits. Locals turned out in force in Diamond Creek, along with lingering tourists. She paused by a back window and looked out over Kachemak Bay. The sun was well on its way down, low over the mountains. Its faded rays mingled with the clouds, shimmering in blurred gold, red and orange on the water.

She turned at a tap on her shoulder. Ethan stood there with a glass of wine held out for her. She grinned and took it, kissing him on the cheek as she did.

"So how are we doing?" she asked.

Ethan winked with a small smile. "Absolutely perfect. I know you had your concerns about opening after summer passed, but we caught the last of the tourists and opening on a First Friday brought half the town out," he said, glancing around at the crowded gallery.

Risa followed his gaze and felt a wave of satisfaction. "I'm pretty happy with how it's gone. Our sales have been fantastic today and tonight's the icing on the cake." She paused to take a sip of wine. "You're right, of course. This will give us the winter to solidify our inventory and head into next summer's tourist season ready to go."

A few customers approached them, and Risa and Ethan separated as they addressed questions. As the evening wore on, Darren kept strolling into Risa's thoughts. It had been two days since he'd been gone, and it was a constant battle not to obsess over him. She alternated between wondering how he was doing and if he was safe to ruminating over her conversation with Hallie and whether she had the nerve to tell him how she felt. She seriously doubted her ability to do that when she could barely stand to consider how she genuinely felt. The word 'love' would rise through her heart, and she had to shove it out of her mind. Restless and irritable, she'd woken this morning with Darren fresh in her thoughts. She'd climbed on her elliptical for a brutal fast-paced workout, an attempt to get him out of her mind. The respite was brief.

As she moved through the gallery, she heard snippets of conversation and came to a complete halt when she heard someone mention that some of the firefighters were unaccounted for today. She didn't want to interrupt, but she was so desperate for information that she stepped to the side of the man who'd spoken and met his eyes when he turned to her.

"I'm sorry to interrupt, but I have a friend who's on one of the crews at the fire. What did you hear?"

The man wasn't bothered by her interruption and continued. "Well, my son who lives in Kenai said that his buddy told him they have three teams that haven't reported back yet today. His buddy is a firefighter from Kenai. They finished their rotation the day before last."

Risa's chest felt tight, her skin clammy. She remained by the group of people while their conversation floated around her. There were various theories about the numerous factors that could have delayed the teams' return. All she could think about was how to find out if Darren had reported back with his team. The man whom she'd overheard appeared to notice her distress and when she turned to move away, he stepped outside the circle of people and placed his hand on her arm.

"I didn't mean to frighten you," he said quietly.

She met his eyes, which were warm blue and kind in his weathered face. She took a shaky breath. "I don't know how to find out if my friend is okay."

"I can have my son call his friend to find out whatever I can for you. Let me do that right now. Don't go anywhere," he said, holding a finger up and stepping to the side of the room.

Risa waited by the counter, trying to stay focused on customers. She answered questions automatically with a polite smile pasted on her face. After a few minutes, the man returned, tucking his phone in his pocket. He rested an elbow against the counter and met her eyes.

"I'm Dan, by the way." His eyes crinkled with his smile.

She nodded jerkily. "I'm Risa."

His kind eyes anchored her. "My son called his friend and called me right back. He said it's not likely they'll give him names yet. They'll want to wait to confirm the situation. Just because the teams haven't reported in doesn't mean they're in danger. With the weather and the vast area where they're spread out, they may have radioed in with a plan to sit tight. In the meantime, he said to call the station here and they'll have any updates for you."

Risa's heart was in her throat, fear coursing through her. She nodded, hot tears pressing against her eyes. She swallowed and took a deep breath. She stumbled through thanking Dan and watched him walk away. The evening was mercifully close to ending. Jack glanced her way and arched a brow. She knew he sensed something, but she was relieved he was too busy to walk over. She couldn't talk about it with the gallery full of people.

She went through the motions until the crowd filtered out of the gallery. Ethan and Jack ushered the last few visitors out the door and locked it. Risa busied herself at the register, tallying up totals and desperate for anything to keep her mind off of Darren.

Ethan walked around the gallery quickly, picking up wineglasses and tidying as he moved through. Jack came to the back and leaned his elbows on the counter.

"Are you okay?" he asked immediately.

The tears she'd been holding at bay spilled over, sliding down her cheeks. She felt ridiculous because she was freaking out and she didn't even know if

Darren was with one of the missing teams. She heard footsteps and then Ethan's voice.

"Oh dear, Jack mentioned he was concerned about you. What's wrong, dear?"

Her shoulders shook, but she forced herself to breathe. A handkerchief appeared in front of her. She snatched it out of Jack's hand and wiped her cheeks.

"I was walking around and overheard some people talking about the fire up north. They said some of the crews hadn't reported in today. Darren's up there with the Diamond Creek crew, and I don't know how to get a hold of him…" Her words tumbled out, stopping when she needed a gulp of air.

She wiped her eyes again and looked up to find two pairs of familiar blue eyes pinned on her with a shared look of concern. Ethan set the tray he held down on the counter and pulled her close for a quick hug. Jack, ever-practical, slipped his phone out of his pocket and made a call. She quickly ascertained he was calling the fire station.

His one-sided conversation did little to soothe her. "When should I call back for another update?" Jack asked before ending the call.

"What did they say?" Risa asked as soon as he moved the phone away from his ear. Ethan's arm remained around her shoulders.

Jack's eyes met hers, his gaze sober. "All they could tell me is two teams that haven't reported back yet are from the Diamond Creek station. They assured me that in a backcountry fire, delayed returns aren't unusual. They did say one team was delayed because they'd rescued a family who took their place on one of the helicopters. That team was accounted for and safe, but waiting for another helicopter to pick them up."

"Did they give you any names? I mean, could they at least tell you who had returned?"

He shook his head. "I'm not family, so no. My suggestion would be to head down there yourself and personally ask. You might get more information that way."

Risa closed her eyes and took a slow breath. She shook her head sharply, trying to force her mind off of its endless loop of unfounded worry. "Okay, okay. Do you guys mind closing up? I'm going to stop by Darren's place and see if his sister knows anything."

Jack and Ethan instantly agreed, but insisted she call them with an update after she talked to Hallie. Ethan assured her they'd be stopping by her place later this evening to check in on her.

* * *

DARREN SAT on the stream bank and glanced around at the sky. The light had faded, stars were winking and a half moon rose behind the mountains. Travis and James lounged beside him. They'd enjoyed a dinner of snack bars and trail mix with water. The helicopter that had been slated to pick them up had been sent to a more pressing pick up. By that point, dusk had settled in with darkness on its way. They'd agreed they could remain for the night and had hunkered down. He wished he could get word to Hallie and Risa, but the best he could hope for was that the station in Diamond Creek would give them an update if they called. Safety wasn't a concern now. The fire was far in the distance now, the shimmering orange from its flames flickering in the dark sky.

When another helicopter carrying water and

flame retardant had passed over earlier, supplies had been dropped for them, which included a deck of cards. They passed the hours until dawn between games of cards and taking turns staying awake in case the wind shifted in their direction again. The cool night air fell around them. Darren rested on his elbows during his time for watch and thought about Risa. He'd give just about anything to be with her right now.

Travis snored nearby while James breathed steadily in the quiet night. The sky was so clear out here it was breathtaking. The smoke was in the distance now, its haze no longer fogging the view. Stars appeared so close, it was as if he could reach out and touch them. He heard a rustling sound and slow footsteps through the burned landscape. He glanced around and saw the shadow of a moose walking on the far side of the stream, the landscape of its home devastated by the fire. Moose thrived on healthy forests. Most of the moose from this area would move to nearby sections of forests. He watched the moose's shadow approach the stream and pause for a drink before lifting its head and turning curiously in their direction. He waited quietly as the moose stared at him in the dark before finally turning away and continuing to follow the stream bank in the direction where the forest was untouched by the fire in the distance.

He couldn't sleep for thoughts of Risa. He needed to find a way to tell her how much she meant to him. Problem was, this was uncharted territory for him. He'd grown so comfortable in the life he'd carved out for himself—a life that didn't involve emotional entanglements and certainly didn't involve putting his heart on the line. But the idea of letting her slip away was terrifying. She was everything he hadn't even known he wanted. Intelligent, kind, funny and so damn sexy it robbed him of his senses. The mixture of bold and vulnerable she carried was intoxicating—so genuine and sexy it took his breath away. And he'd left with the intent to wash her out of his mind. Instead, she'd burrowed in under his defenses and he couldn't shake free, nor did he want to anymore. And for now, he had to wait through the night and hope he could call her in the morning.

* * *

RISA SAT in Darren's living room with Hallie, Ethan and Jack. After she'd arrived at Darren's house to discover Hallie frantic because she hadn't received the daily call Darren promised her when he got in, Risa had decided to stay with her. She didn't want Hallie to worry alone. After Ethan called to check on her, he and Jack had driven over to Darren's house with pizza from Glacier Pizza, her favorite local pizza place.

They'd finished eating hours ago. Darkness had fallen. Stars winked bright against the bare sky, and a half moon glittered above the mountains, the water in the bay shimmering in its bright light. She and Hallie were seated together on one side of the sectional while Ethan and Jack sat on the other corner. The television rumbled while Jack dealt cards. He and Ethan had insisted they were staying to force her and Hallie not to obsess about Darren when there was nothing else to do. Hallie had been able to get information from the station that Darren was on one of the teams that hadn't reported in, but they confirmed he was safe and waiting with his team until daylight to be flown out.

Risa wasn't satisfied with that answer. It helped to know something, but the anxiety knotted in her chest and stomach wouldn't ease until she knew for certain he was out of the fire zone. She glanced up when Jack said her name.

"What?" she asked.

He rolled his eyes. "Your turn."

"Oh, right." She quickly laid a card down.

Hallie glanced at her and over to Ethan and Jack. "So, I told Risa she needs to tell Darren how she feels? Don't you think?"

Ethan chuckled. "Honey, we suggested that weeks ago. Risa seems to be taking her sweet time with it."

Risa glared at him. "I wasn't sure how I felt. Now I'm a little more sure, but I still don't know what Darren thinks. I mean, he didn't even bother to tell me about this trip ahead of time. He left me a message the night before he left town."

Doubts were hunkered down in her brain. Her feelings had already run roughshod over her intellect when it came to Darren. His strong, quiet, reserved routine didn't help her feel more confident. Here she was obsessing over his safety, almost out of her mind with worry and for all she knew, he wasn't even thinking about her.

Hallie wagged her finger at her. "I already told you I know Darren. He's got it bad for you. Seriously bad. He needs something to shake him up enough to stop being so careful."

Risa took a sip of water and set the glass down on the coffee table with a sigh. "Right, well I just don't want to be the idiot again."

Ethan and Jack collectively sighed and turned their eyes to her. Ethan spoke. "I met Darren and while I won't claim to know him the way Hallie does, he's no Brad. Brad was a shallow fool. Whatever happens with Darren, he's not out to treat you like that. I know it."

Hallie nodded emphatically, though she had no idea who Brad was. After a few more minutes of this, Risa managed to outlast them and the conversation moved on. She eventually nodded off on the couch, the last thought on her mind was Darren—wondering how he was doing out in the backcountry in the chilly fall night.

CHAPTER 23

Dawn followed the sun as its rays spread from behind the mountains. Frost coated the ground, making the burned landscape look ghostly with a soft fuzz of glittery white atop the charred surface. Steam rose in the air as the sun crested the mountains and hit the frost, quickly melting it. A mist floated as far as the eye could see as the sun rose further in the sky. Darren had never managed to fall asleep and stood to stretch and look around. When Travis had woken for his round of watch, Darren had shaken his head and told him it was no bother. He'd known he wouldn't be able to sleep—not with his mind circling on Risa and those long moments when he'd raced back into the house for the little girl. He was chilly and stiff from the night. Sleeping bags had been dropped with their supplies, so he quickly rolled up the one he'd rested in while he watched the night go by. He could no longer see the fire in the distance, only lingering streaks of smoke along the horizon. Risa had drifted in and out of his thoughts throughout the long night. This morning, he was determined to call her as soon as he could, so he could hear her voice. He had far more to say than that, but he hadn't quite sorted that out.

He tugged his phone out of his pocket and strode to a small rise nearby, hoping he could get some phone reception. The icon on his screen indicated no reception…still. With a sigh, he put his phone away and walked to the stream, splashing cold water on his face. He turned to look over at Travis and James, both zipped tight in their sleeping bags and dead to the world. He started organizing his gear and had a snack bar while he waited for them to wake up. He figured there was no sense in forcing them to get up when they had nowhere to go until the helicopter arrived. When he heard the muffled sound of the radio, he sifted through Travis' bag and pulled it out.

He confirmed their location and received notice that the helicopter was estimated to reach them within a half hour. Travis lifted his head, his eyes bleary. "Did I just hear we're about to get picked up?" he said groggily.

"Half hour. I'd say it's time to rise and shine," Darren replied.

Travis promptly fell back with a groan, but immediately sat up again, shaking his head sharply. Darren walked over and shook James to wake him. They were ready to roll by the time they heard the helicopter in the distance. When he climbed aboard, Darren leaned back with a sigh in his seat and accepted a thermos of coffee handed over by one of the pilots. After a few sips of bracing black coffee, he thought he could make it through the day. His mind may not have been able to turn off last night, but his body was exhausted.

When they landed at the closest helipad in Kenai, they were shuttled over to the staging area on the outskirts of the area where the fire had started. Tents fluttered in the chilly breeze with breakfast set up at a small buffet. After piling his plate high with eggs, bacon and toast, he sat down at a long table and finally checked his phone. Still no reception. He knew Hallie would be worried because he'd assured her he'd call every night he could. She knew to check with the station if she didn't hear from him, but he could only hope she'd gotten the word that he was safe and sound. He also hoped she'd have called Risa. It bothered him that he hadn't spoken to Risa the night before he left now. When he'd left the message, he'd felt relieved that he could just tell her he'd be out of town for a few days. He'd hoped it would shake the spell she'd put him under. Now he only hoped his carelessness hadn't pushed her further away. She was skittish enough as it was.

Most of their crew had returned, but they found out that one team remained unaccounted for—including two full-time firefighters from Diamond Creek and another back-up firefighter like him. Unlike his team, no one had been able to reach this team yet. The helicopter that had been intended to pick them up and changed routes had done a fly over yesterday evening with no sign of them. Darren's stomach knotted while he waited with the rest of the crew. He was friends with every one of the guys, but he knew the full-timers were really tight. It was how he was with his police partners. When you faced danger every day and had to count on each other, the bond was strong—whether it was ever expressed in words or not. Not knowing where these guys were was tearing at the heart of this crew.

By early afternoon, there was still no word. Rescue crews were out there tracking where the fire had moved to try to assess where the team was. Darren and the rest of the Diamond Creek crew weren't cleared to return to the field and would be sent home this afternoon. Darren had managed to get to a brief moment of crappy reception by standing on top of one of the trucks. He'd left Hallie and Risa messages. He'd radioed to the station and asked them to call as well.

Hours later on the ride home to Diamond Creek, they received a call reporting that the missing team had been located. Two of the guys from the team had gotten caught off guard when the wind changed direction. Both survived, but one was in bad shape. They'd been driven down into a small valley by the fire, which is why the helicopter hadn't seen them yesterday evening. The only one who wasn't injured had remained with the team to do what he could to stabilize them with emergency medical supplies. All three had been picked up and flown to the hospital in Anchorage for clearance.

As Darren rode home with Travis, Travis glanced over, his eyes assessing. "So did I hear you ask the station to call Risa?"

Darren shrugged. "So what?"

"Since when was Risa so important that she lands on the list of family for updates?"

Darren shifted his shoulders and rolled his head from side to side, easing the tension in his neck. He glanced out the passenger window. Cook Inlet stretched ahead in the view, the mountains rising tall on the far side. Gulls coasted in the soft breeze over the water, which glittered under the bright sun. With a sigh he looked back at Travis whose gaze was on the road again.

"Since I can't seem to get her out of my mind," Darren said bluntly.

"Does this mean you two are serious because I gotta give it to you if you are. You have seriously played your cards close. I knew you were into her, and I'd heard here and there you two were sort of seeing each other, but that's about it."

Darren chewed on the inside of his mouth and considered Travis' words. He had played his cards close to his chest. Because he hadn't wanted anyone, including Risa, to think too much of his actions and read into them.

"How about this? We haven't been serious in the sense that we've discussed it, but spending the night in a burned forest puts things in perspective. I can't stop thinking about her, so I figure I'd better face the fact that I'd like to make it serious."

Travis nodded, smiling wryly. "Fair enough."

They were quiet after that, and they rode home to Diamond Creek through a glorious fall afternoon, yellow birch leaves floating in the wind. Thrumming in the background was the underlying fear and concern for how the rescued crewmembers were faring.

* * *

AT THE GALLERY, Risa entered inventory pricing on a spreadsheet, losing focus repeatedly as her mind wandered to Darren. After she'd woken this morning on

Darren's couch, Risa had joined Hallie for coffee and then headed home to shower and change. Ethan and Jack were already at the gallery when she arrived, busy planning and cleaning up from the opening event. Risa had failed miserably at keeping her thoughts off of Darren. He'd left a message this morning when she was in the shower, reporting through a poor, broken connection that he was back at the base camp and would call later when he had a better connection. Knowing he was safe seemed to only stir the stew of her thoughts.

Shortly after his message, she'd received a message from the fire station that he had reported in and would be returning from duty this afternoon. The message had indicated he'd requested she be contacted for updates due to his poor connection. She was restless and had trouble concentrating. So, he couldn't be bothered to actually let her know his plans other than a passing phone call, but now he wanted to make sure she was kept up to date. She'd spent the night worrying about him, wondering if she had the courage to talk to him about how she felt, and now she could barely consider it. Her nerves were worn thin and frazzled by a poor night's sleep.

Risa went through the motions of work, somehow managing to talk to customers though her mind was only half present. Ethan and Jack left for lunch, and she sold a few pieces. The most recent customer had left when the doorbell chimed. She glanced up to see Emma and Trey entering the gallery, Stuart walking between them.

"Aunt Risa!" Stuart raced to her, colliding with her in an enthusiastic hug.

"Hey buddy!" Risa swept him in her arms for a

kiss, quickly setting him back down. She looked up to Emma and Trey. "Hey there, glad you could make it." She gestured around the gallery. "Take a look around. Where's Janet?"

Trey tugged her in for a quick hug. "We dropped her off with Hannah for the afternoon." He glanced around. "It looks great. How'd last night go?"

Emma had already started meandering through the gallery. Risa updated them on the opening night as they checked out the new displays. She hesitated to explain what happened with Darren. She and Trey had yet to discuss her relationship with Darren and with Stuart here, she didn't think it was the best timing. Their visit was a distraction, but her mind kept wandering back to Darren. As if she'd conjured him, she looked out the front window and saw his patrol car pull up out front. She'd figured he'd arrive in Diamond Creek sometimes this afternoon, but had expected a call, not an unannounced visit to the gallery. Her heart flew to her throat. She wasn't ready to see him, not like this. Though Emma and Trey were a friendly audience, her feelings were too raw. Stuart would be a font of questions, and she wasn't ready to fall apart in front of everyone.

She watched Darren walk through the parking lot and up the steps. His shoulders were hunched. He lifted his head as he stepped through the door, his eyes meeting hers. Emotion barreled through her at such a force she had to close her eyes and brace herself. She'd been so scared for him, hours and hours of worry and waiting. And here he was. Safe and sound. His chocolate eyes were trained on her the second she opened hers again. His eyes held a question, but she didn't dare do anything other than try to keep things light.

Emma came around from behind one of the displays. "Darren! So good to see you," she said, walking to his side.

Darren returned her greeting, his eyes finally breaking from Risa's.

Trey turned from where he stood, joining Emma beside Darren. "Hey Darren!" Trey clapped him on his shoulder. "Good to see you. Heard you were up with the Diamond Creek crew at the fire and got held up last night. Can't tell you how glad I was to hear everyone's okay."

Darren looked slightly dazed, but he accepted Trey's greeting, his smile muted. "Thanks, man. Good to be here. Wish I could say everyone's back, but we're still waiting for word on Ed and Mike from the hospital in Anchorage."

Cold anxiety coursed through Risa. Darren could have been one of those men. Instead, he stood in front of them, his eyes weary and blood-shot, the lingering scent of smoke clinging to him...but strong and safe. His eyes held deep worry and concern. She wanted to hug him close and tell him somehow his friends would be okay. But she couldn't do that, not here. She met his eyes, trying to convey her feelings in a long glance.

Stuart slipped between his parents and grinned up at Darren. "Hey! Aren't you a police officer?"

Risa watched Darren paste on his public face as he knelt down and shook Stuart's hand.

"You smell like a fire!" Stuart exclaimed.

"Well, that's because I've been out in the middle of one," Darren replied with a wry grin.

This elicited a host of questions from Stuart. Risa looked on, emotions tumbling through her. She desperately wished for a few minutes alone with Darren, but she clearly wasn't going to get them right now.

Ethan and Jack came through the door. Ethan's blue eyes met hers. He gave a tiny shrug and stepped to Darren's side first.

"Darren, so good to see you. We met your lovely sister last night. She and Risa were so worried about you. We're glad to see you made it home safe and sound," he said smoothly. He laid his hand lightly on Darren's shoulder.

Darren's eyes traveled to hers repeatedly as he stood and chatted politely with everyone. She somehow managed to join the conversation, but she kept it brief and busied herself at the counter with pointless tasks. Between the fact that their relationship wasn't on clear grounds and certainly wasn't public, she felt out of place. Her emotions were roiling. Emma caught her eyes, appearing to sense her distress. Risa shook her head when Emma moved to follow her.

Ethan excused himself and came to her side. "Dear, it's obvious you're uncomfortable. Shall we find a way to clear the gallery?" he asked. "I'm guessing you'd like some time to yourself with him."

Risa looked over at Darren. Stuart was tugging on his hand, asking him another question. Emma put her hands on Stuart's shoulders and said something in his ear. Darren glanced to her. She couldn't read his expression. Before she replied to Ethan, she heard Darren tell the others he had to get going. With a quick wave, he left. It took most of her will not to burst into tears. He hadn't done anything wrong. It had simply been an inconvenient moment to stop by. With her emotions frayed, she hadn't wanted to have a meltdown in front of her family and friends.

She met Ethan's eyes, blinking back tears. "Another time," she said around the lump in her throat.

She strode from behind the counter and whirled Stuart up in her arms. "Hey buddy, so tell me when we can have one of our beach walks again?"

As Stuart giggled, Risa met Emma's eyes. Emma looked worried, but Risa ignored her, spinning around with Stuart. Moments later, after a plan was confirmed for a walk in the next few days, Emma and Trey left with Stuart.

Risa walked to the back of the gallery and slipped into the office, closing the door behind her. Sitting down in the desk chair, she rested her elbows on the desk, her face in her hands. Hot tears pricked behind her eyes. Her throat was tight. Quiet settled around her. She finally lifted her head and glanced out the window, which faced Kachemak Bay. The tiny slice of a view offered a straight line of sight to one of the glaciers in a valley between mountain peaks. Sun glinted off its translucent blue surface. Snow had fallen last night. The peaks of the mountains were bright white in the sun. An eagle screeched nearby and flew past the window, landing on a piece of drift-wood on the beach. She'd heard that a pod of beluga whales had been out in the bay yesterday. She scanned the water, hoping to see them. For now, the bay hid its residents under its wind-ruffled surface. She looked away with a sigh.

So that was great, just great. You're supposed to be

getting up the nerve to tell him you think you've fallen in love with him, and now he probably thinks you don't even care.

Then there was the fact that her heart clenched at the sight of him, to see him and know he was really, really okay. She'd heard what the station said earlier when they called. She'd heard his message, but her heart had still been tight, anxiety a knot in her chest. She wanted to see him. And she had—with a well-intended audience. She sighed and leaned back in her chair, absently lifting up a small hourglass with colored sand and turning it over, watching the sand slowly mark time.

There was a soft knock at the door. Jack glanced around the corner. She tried to smile, but her effort wobbled. She waved him in.

He sat across from her, his eyes assessing. "I'm guessing you'd have liked a few minutes to yourself with Darren," he said with a soft chuckle.

Risa shrugged. "Probably."

Jack leaned back. "Your Darren could hardly keep his eyes off of you."

"He's not my Darren."

Jack arched a brow. "I beg to differ. Don't tell me you're going to stick to that line after last night?"

Risa bit her lip and glared at him. "Don't give me a hard time. I'm so tied up in knots, I can't even think straight."

Jack's expression softened. "I wasn't trying to give you a hard time. But I don't think pretending he doesn't matter will help. You're clearly in love with him, so perhaps now would be a good time to make sure he knows that."

"Now would be a good time to hide under a rock."

Jack threw his head back with a laugh. He met her eyes again. "Avoiding him isn't going to resolve this. He came to see you, why don't you go see him now?"

Risa shrugged and didn't reply. She wasn't accustomed to feeling this out of control. It was bad enough to try to scrounge up the courage to tell Darren how she felt and worse when she hadn't counted on how hard it would be to manage the hurricane of her emotions in his presence.

Ethan poked his head around the door. "Hey, could use a little help out here."

Risa started to stand up. Ethan waved for her to sit down again. "Not you. You're excused. Get on the phone and call your boyfriend. Jack can help me."

Jack stood up and grinned. "Do what Ethan said," he said pointedly before striding out of the office. She heard their muted voices talking with customers and twirled her chair around to face the window again. The sun glinted off the waves rolling into shore. As she looked out across the bay, she suddenly stood. Sleek white curves flashed atop the waves and back under the water—the pod of beluga whales she'd heard about. They traveled along Cook Inlet and into the bay every so often. Even from a distance, she was in awe. They were so white against the slate gray water, moving in unison in a rippling pod across the water. She watched them until they disappeared from sight, diving down together into the depths of the bay.

CHAPTER 24

*D*arren walked across the station parking lot on the way back to his car. A biting wind blew straight into his face. The blink of fall in Alaska was almost over. The white line of snow on the mountains across the bay got lower every morning. He expected snow to fly at sea level any day now and wouldn't be surprised if Diamond Creek woke to a thin layer of snow after this evening. He kept his head down and swiftly climbed into his truck. The cessation of wind was so welcome, he sighed in relief. The wind whistled around his truck, but the cab was still and quiet.

His phone buzzed. He shifted to tug it out of his pocket. Risa's name flashed on the screen. He hit silent and set it on the dashboard. He hadn't spoken to her since he'd stopped by the gallery yesterday. She'd left him a message and called another time last night. He knew she wanted to talk, but he wasn't quite sure he was ready for that. He'd gotten himself all worked up to walk into the gallery and tell her that she mattered, really mattered, to him yesterday. His plans had evaporated when he found her there with Trey and Emma, her nephew busy peppering him with questions. He'd had to swallow his feelings and put on his public face. He'd left the gallery thrown off and discombobulated.

He missed her like hell and wanted to call her back, but his emotional state after his long night in the backcountry wasn't helping. It had taken all of the tattered threads of his nerves to convince himself it was worth it to let go and move past his self-imposed boundaries around relationships. He drove home, trying and failing to keep his mind off of Risa.

Hours later, Hallie glared at him across the kitchen counter.

"What the hell is wrong with you?"

"Damn Hallie, cut me some slack."

Hallie put her hands on her hips and shook her head, her ponytail bouncing. "You obviously want to talk to Risa, and you ignored her call. I saw her name on the screen. And don't go acting like I'm being nosy. If you don't want me to notice anything on your phone, don't leave it on the counter right beside me. I looked down without even thinking. She was here all night the other night while we were waiting for word on you. I don't know what your problem is, but ignoring calls is a jerk move."

Darren turned on his heel and walked to the couch, throwing himself down and kicking his feet up on the coffee table. He knew Hallie had a point, but he wasn't up for arguing with her. He grabbed the remote and turned on the television.

Hallie followed him over and stood in front of him, blocking his view. "Well, if you won't bother calling her, I will. The least you could do is let her know you're okay."

"She knows I'm okay. She saw me yesterday." As soon as the words left his mouth, he realized he'd opened himself up to a line of questioning from Hallie.

"You saw her yesterday? When?"

"I stopped by her gallery after I got back." He tried to hew to the facts without giving her too much to run with.

"And?"

"And what?"

"Oh my God! You're purposefully being obtuse. Which tells me you're avoiding something. Spill it. I'm your sister. I tell you practically everything."

Darren leaned his head against the couch and closed his eyes. The nightly news droned in the background. He opened his eyes and looked at Hallie. "I stopped by her gallery to see her. You'll be happy to know, I got myself all worked up to, I don't know, try to tell her she meant something to me. Not to be corny, but I had a lot of time to think while I was out working the fire the last few days."

Hallie's eyes brightened when he paused.

He lifted his brows in return.

"So then what?" she asked.

"I left."

"You left?"

"That's what I said," he replied.

"But why?"

"Because her family was there, along with her two bosses. It wasn't the time or place to talk, so I left."

Hallie just kept looking at him as if expecting him to offer more. Darren inwardly groaned. Hallie wasn't going to stop asking questions until he explained his thought process. Much it annoyed the hell out of him sometimes, she knew him well enough to know when he was putting her off.

"Hallie, I get it. You want me to be with Risa. Isn't it enough that I've been seeing her?"

Hallie stepped away and flung herself on the other side of the sectional. "Seriously? You're being ridiculous." Her tone was loaded with exasperation.

Hallie's pressure only increased the internal pressure he felt. He closed his eyes and took a slow breath.

Hallie's expression softened. "You're scared."

Darren's chest tightened at her words. "Maybe I am. Could you please let me go at my own pace here? You know this is a new thing for me. I wrote off relationships after the accident. The fact that I'm even contemplating this is a big deal."

Hallie quieted and didn't comment again. She looked out the window.

Darren flipped the remote around in his hand. "I'll call her back tonight."

Hallie let the topic drop to his relief. After she meandered off to the guest room later, he retrieved the phone from the kitchen counter and called Risa. He got her voice mail. Though he hated admitting it, he knew Hallie had a point. Not answering her calls was a jerk move, even if the only reason he was avoiding her was that his feelings for her scared him half out of his mind. So he took a deep breath and left a message. And asked her to call him back. And told her he was sorry he hadn't called yet. And told her he missed her.

And the sky didn't fall.

* * *

Risa was up early and put herself through another grueling bout on her elliptical. She hadn't been sleeping well and needed something to burn off the restless energy she couldn't seem to shake. She'd forced herself to turn her phone off last night after she'd tried calling Darren again only to get no answer. Three calls and two messages was enough. More than that and she would feel like she was stalking him and clearly not taking a hint. After she showered, she finally turned her phone on. Her heart flew to her throat when she saw he'd called late last night.

His voice was gravelly, but his words were heaven. He went so far as to say he was sorry he hadn't called...and *he missed her.* She replayed his message about ten times. He paused before he said he missed her. She could hear the breath he took before he said it, as if he was gathering courage. She did a little happy dance in her living room, holding her phone close to her chest. It was on the early side, but she called him back anyway. She was so giddy, she wasn't even disappointed when she got his voice message. Feeling bold, she asked him to stop by the gallery if he could today.

Hours later, she strode down the short hallway in the back of the gallery to the office. Ethan and Jack were still here helping out for the week, so she had the freedom to take a break from the floor. Her feet were sore from a new pair of heels she'd worn, so she sat down at her desk, immediately kicking her shoes off. She whirled the chair around to look out the window. Ever since she'd seen the beluga whales the other day, she was constantly scanning the bay for another glimpse. The sun struck sparks off the glacier. The snow that dusted the peaks had made its way further down the flanks of the mountains during the night. Wind gusted across the water, stirring whitecaps in its wake.

There was a quick knock on the door. She called out for whomever it was to come in, assuming it was Ethan or Jack.

The door opened and closed quietly. "Hey Risa."

At the sound of Darren's voice, she whirled around. She didn't hesitate and raced around the desk, flinging her arms around his neck. His arms came around her and lifted her in his embrace. She leaned back and looked into his warm chocolate eyes. He still looked weary, but his gaze was open and zeroed in on her. She cupped his cheek with her hand.

"It's *so* good to see you." Emotion washed over her in a wave as she looked into his eyes. Whatever it was between them, she wasn't going to be a coward and wait and see if he felt the way she did. She was going to trust what she felt and that he would be on this path with her however they navigated it.

"I missed you. A lot," she said bluntly.

"I missed you. A lot." He mimicked her words with a grin.

His arms loosened and she slid down his body to the floor, savoring the feel of his hard body against hers. She took a step back and leaned against her desk. She didn't know how to proceed other than to simply say what she felt.

"I don't know what you're thinking or feeling, but I don't want to waste any more time without telling you what's happening for me. This," she gestured between them. "...thing between us. It's way more than I bargained on. When I met you, well, let's just say there was some chemistry. But I haven't had the best luck with relationships." She paused to gauge his response.

He merely arched a brow.

"Not that it matters, but I was giving some perspective. Anyway, so I thought I'd have some fun with you. But right from the start, you blew me away. I can't stop thinking about you. I miss you when I'm not with you, and I don't want this to be something that goes away because we're both trying to play it cool. So I'm done playing it cool. I don't know if you want to give something more a shot, but if you do, I hope you might with me."

When she finished speaking, anxiety swirled in her belly. She'd never so blatantly put her heart on the line like that. Her heart galloped in her chest. It was exhilarating and terrifying. Holding her breath, she met Darren's eyes. He took two strides to reach her, lifting a hand to tuck a loose lock of hair behind her ear. A shiver raced through her at his soft touch.

His eyes were trained on hers. His shoulders rose and fell with a deep breath. "I couldn't bear it if I thought I couldn't see you again. I missed you so much the last few days, my brain was a broken record. All I want is you."

His words were direct, his voice husked with need. His chocolate gaze darkened as he held her eyes. He traced her mouth, pausing on her lower lip, the pad of his thumb resting there. Heat pooled in her center, desire unfurling within and coursing through her body. In a breath, the air around them came to life, vibrating with the pulse of passion that thrummed between them whenever they were near. Her pulse skittered, her breath became shallow. He murmured her name, eliciting a quiver in her belly. He leaned forward in slow motion, his lips meeting hers softly for a moment and then claiming her mouth fiercely.

Risa slipped a hand around his neck and pulled him closer. Darren's hand fell away from her mouth, his warm strong hands sliding down her sides, lingering on her curves before cupping her bottom and lifting her onto the desk. Her fitted skirt rode up around her hips as he stepped between her knees, tugging her close against him. Arousal spiked through her. She couldn't get close enough, wrapping her legs around his hips and running her hands up the muscled planes of his chest.

Their kiss was hot, wet and devastating. When he tore his lips away and blazed a wet trail down her neck, she gasped for air. He tore at her blouse. When the buttons caught, he swore and yanked, the fabric tearing. Cool air hit her flushed skin, her nipples pebbling under the thin silk of her bra. With a flick of his thumb, her bra came undone, her breasts spilling out, hot and aching for his touch. His breath hissed through his teeth. His eyes met hers, and she melted in the heat of his dark brown gaze. Holding her eyes, he lifted his hand, grazing it across her nipples, the barest touch tightening the coil of desire within her.

There was a sharp knock at the door. Darren stepped away quickly, his eyes locked onto hers as he stepped backward to the door, reaching to lock it. He shrugged his jacket off, letting it fall to the floor. Footsteps retreated away from the door down the hall. Darren moved swiftly, his hot, warm, hard body nestled in the cradle of her hips in a breath. His hips rocked into her, tiny spikes of pleasure coursed through her. She was drenched with want for him. She shoved his shirt up, desperate for the feel of his skin against hers. He reached behind his neck and pulled his t-shirt up and over his head at once. She moaned in relief when his warm, muscled chest pressed against her breasts.

He feathered kisses across her face, down her neck and across the tops of her breasts, hot sparks of electricity sizzling with each touch of his lips on her skin. She slid her hands up over his muscled chest and around his back, scoring his skin with her nails when his mouth closed around her nipple. He drew it deeply into his mouth, the bite of his teeth a balm. The sharp pain relieved her desperation, if only for a second.

Darren murmured her name when he lifted his head. He toyed with her nipples, rolling them between his fingers, tugging lightly when she arched into his touch. Releasing her nipples, he stepped back and clasped her calves. She closed her eyes at the feel of his strong hands, their heat traveling in a tantalizing path up her legs, pushing her thighs further apart, his thumbs coming to rest at the apex. The silk there was wet with the evidence of her desire. He stroked his thumb slowly back and forth across the silk. Her hips shifted restlessly into his touch. Her breath came in ragged gasps.

He slipped a finger under the edge of her panties and finally delved into her folds, slick with want. Another finger joined the first as he slowly drove her mad with light touches and deep plunges.

"Risa..." he whispered.

She dragged her eyes open, instantly lost in his intense gaze. She bit her lip to keep from crying out as he caressed over and around her clit. She clenched around his fingers, the tremors building inside until she burst, the force of her climax rolling through her so rapidly her breath went out in a rush. His lips came against hers just as she cried out, muffling the sound. He eased his strokes as the vibrations slowed within her. He pulled his hand away, lifting his head.

Dazed with passion, she met his eyes, still brimming with desire, the aftermath of her climax thrumming through her. Holding his gaze, she tore at his jeans, swiftly freeing his cock, wrapping her hand around his hot velvet skin. He groaned at her touch.

"Risa, you don't have to…"

She put her finger to his lips.

"I want to."

She shifted her hips closer, so she was half off the desk, and guided him into her slick channel. In a swift surge, he sheathed himself to the hilt, settling against her with such force it took her breath away. His eyes closed and he took a deep breath. He opened his eyes, his forehead falling against hers. He began a rhythm of slow, deep strokes. She met him stroke for stroke, the reverberations from her lingering orgasm building into another one, the depth and intensity of it washing over her in a crashing wave. As soon her channel began to clench and pulse around him, he surged deeply one final time, spilling himself inside of her. They came silently, their breath mingling in quiet, broken gasps.

They stayed like that for long moments, Darren's head bowed against hers, his lips inches from hers. The distant sound of the entry chime finally filtered through Risa's awareness. When she lifted her head, his followed, though he remained inside of her.

"Well…" she said softly.

Darren's mouth kicked up at the corner. "Right."

She giggled. "So how am I supposed to go back to work?"

She gestured at her torn blouse. He tilted his head, a slow smile spreading across his face, completely unapologetic.

"You can wear my jacket," he offered helpfully.

She swatted at his chest. "It's a good thing Ethan and Jack will be thrilled to learn I got some action from you today."

He arched a brow. "I can see they probably wouldn't care one way or another, but they have an opinion on us?"

She nodded vigorously, finally shifting her hips slightly. He slowly stepped back, pulling out of her and glancing around. She snagged the box of tissues on her desk and handed it to him with a smile. He wiped himself off and then her. As she wiggled off her desk, she glanced up at him.

"Yes, they have an opinion about us. They've been on my case to talk to you for a few weeks now."

He zipped his pants and grabbed his t-shirt off the floor. His voice was muffled as the fabric fell over his head. "You mean, we could have taken care of this weeks ago?"

When his face reappeared, she held his gaze and took a deep breath. "Yeah. I had to work up the nerve. Ethan says I have 'issues' with intimacy. Don't push me on that just yet, saying what I already said was a big deal for me."

He smiled wryly, warmth and understanding in his eyes. "I'm thinking I should thank them." He paused, his gaze sobering. "So you know, Hallie might say I have 'issues' with intimacy too."

Risa giggled. "I won't hold it against you." She looked down at her torn blouse and tugged her bra together. "Now seriously, I can't go out like this. I'm going to have to call it a day and borrow your jacket on my way out."

He swept it up from the floor and walked over, dropping in on her shoulders. Slipping her arms in it, she tugged it around her, savoring the scent of him on it. There was a knock on the door again. This time, Darren stepped to the door and opened it. Ethan stood on the other side, his eyes warm with a knowing smile.

He looked over them both, taking in Darren's jacket wrapped around Risa and her rumpled appearance. "We're sending you home for the day." He glanced at Darren. "I'd say thank you, but that might seem strange," he offered with a grin.

Darren shrugged and gestured to Risa. She stepped to his side and walked out, his arm securely around her shoulders.

CHAPTER 25

*D*arren sat up abruptly, jolted awake. His skin was damp and his breathing ragged. Risa lay beside him, curled up under the covers. Moonlight splashed across the bed through the windows. He waited for his breathing to slow down and his heart to stop racing. He didn't realize she was awake until he felt her hand reach up and curl around his shoulder, stroking down his arm in a warm, soothing caress.

"It's snowing," she said, her voice soft and filled with wonder in the darkness.

He looked over at her to see she was looking up into the skylight over the bed. The snowflakes were lit up in the bright moonlight, falling like glittering fairy dust. He shifted and lay back down, resting beside her and watching the snow fall, dreamlike in the quiet night. She curled against his side, her legs tangling with his, her head on his shoulder. A time that was usually filled with dread and rumination for him wasn't that at all. His heartbeat slowed to normal, her hand traced circles on his chest.

He fell back asleep and woke hours later, sunlight splashing across the bed. The shower was running and Risa wasn't in bed. He rolled out of bed and walked into the shower, sliding his hands around her soft curves and nuzzling her neck.

"Mmm, good morning," she said.

"Mmm…" was all he could manage.

She turned in his arms and met his eyes, hers crinkling with a smile. "Breakfast?"

The haze of sleep not quite out of his head, he must have looked confused.

"Do you want me to make breakfast?" she asked slowly.

"Oh sure."

She grinned and pecked him on the cheek before shimmying around him to step out of the shower. He quickly soaped himself and rinsed. By the time he was dressed, the entire house smelled like bacon. He entered the kitchen to find Hallie sitting at the counter chatting with Risa. Risa handed him a fresh cup of coffee and gestured for him to sit at the counter.

Hallie eyed him over the rim of her mug, her eyes smiling.

"Morning Hallie. Didn't know you were here this morning," he commented.

"I'm guessing you didn't notice I was home last night when you got here," she said with a sly grin as she took a sip of coffee and set her mug down.

He definitely hadn't noticed, wrapped in the fog of Risa as he'd been. He shrugged and returned her grin.

Risa served them breakfast and then left for work

in a swirl. "I have a ton of stuff to get caught up on since I left early yesterday," she said as she tugged her jacket on.

They'd stopped by her apartment yesterday afternoon, so she could pick up some clothes. Though Darren enjoyed watching her wear his jacket, he knew it didn't fit her style or sensibility.

She glanced at him, her brown eyes bright and warm. "Are we having dinner together?"

"Yes," he replied swiftly with absolutely no hesitation.

Her return smile was brighter than the sun—at least to him. "I'll text you later about when and where," she said, giving him a quick kiss.

When she swung the door open, brisk air blew in, scented with snow. A thin layer of snow coated everything in sight. Where the sun struck, it sparkled as it melted almost instantly. Darren stepped into his boots and followed her out, grabbing the snowbrush out of his car. He quickly brushed the snow off her windshield. When he finished, he looked up to find her staring at him.

"What?"

She shook her head sharply and stepped to his side, flinging her arms around him. His came around her reflexively. She hugged him tightly and leaned back to look at him. "Just that you're too good, much too good of a man," she said with a soft smile.

He was puzzled but happily accepted her kiss, this one much more than the peck she'd given him at the door. By the time she pulled away, his pulse was pounding, lust was streaking through him, and he needed a cold shower.

* * *

RISA FOLLOWED the boardwalk around the back of the gallery and assorted storefronts. She shivered when a bracing gust of salty wind came from the bay. Tugging her jacket more tightly around her, she leaned on the railing and looked out over the water. It was early evening with the sky navy, almost dark, but not quite. The long summer days were gone. Time quickened during autumn in Alaska, racing toward winter. The mountains across the bay were bathed in alpenglow, lingering light from the fallen sun bouncing off the water and snow on the peaks to create a soft lavender mist along the horizon.

A raven flew by and landed on the railing nearby, offering her a cursory glance before commencing to stare out over the water. The tide was rolling out, the waves lapping softly on the shore, the briny scent from tide pools carrying on the breeze. Risa took a deep breath, the chilly autumn ocean air energizing and soothing at once. She thought about yesterday with Darren and couldn't have stopped the smile that spread across her face if she'd tried. For the first time in as long as she could recall, she wasn't second-guessing herself. Oh, it helped for Darren to respond as he did and blow her away again, but it felt so good, so right to simply speak what she felt aloud instead of keeping it bottled up inside for fear of what might happen.

The early hours of this morning had been an unexpected gift. When he'd woken after another nightmare, she'd expected him to head for the shower as he always had. Instead, he'd watched the snow flutter onto the skylight with her and fallen back asleep quickly. She'd been awake longer than he, listening to his breath tumble into the lull of sleep.

Glancing at her watch, she took a last look out over the water. A seal rose up by the shore, its large round eyes staring at her curiously. With a wave to the seal, she turned and walked to her car. She was meeting Darren for dinner at The Boathouse Café. If it were summer, she'd have walked, but the autumn breeze had too much bite to it. She drove the short distance from the gallery to The Boathouse, which was on one of the bluffs near Otter Cove Harbor.

Entering the restaurant, she took a look around. The café was an updated diner with the grill area visible behind a counter with seating. The walls were lined with the original booths with updated tabletops of mahogany and crisp white place mats. Brightly colored curtains offered a splash of color and cheer. As her eyes traveled around, she saw Darren already seated in a booth in the corner and made her way over there.

Startling her, he stood and leaned in for a kiss when she reached the booth. As was always the case with him, passion simmered on high idle. What she'd assumed would be a quick kiss was more than that, his tongue sweeping quickly inside her mouth, his teeth catching at her bottom lip and tugging swiftly before he pulled back. Desire flushed her skin. Flustered, she slid into the booth, pulling her jacket off and setting it beside her. Looking up, she met his eyes, his warm chocolate gaze honed in on her.

"Hey," he said with a grin.

"Hey yourself. How was your day?"

He shrugged, twirling his beer bottle in his hand. "Nothing unusual. This time of year tends to feel slow because we're coming off the tourist season. We spend summer responding to wild parties and dealing with a population that quadruples. Today, I caught up on reports and responded to a call about a moose in the high school parking lot."

"And what happened to the moose?"

"We herded him out of the parking lot and into the woods nearby. No harm done. How was your day?"

Risa filled him in on the gallery happenings. She soaked in how nice it felt to have someone to talk to about her day. Aside from the fact that his mere presence stole her breath and set her pulse galloping, Darren was warm and kind, legitimately interested in her daily life. As she waited while someone stopped by the table to chat with him, a fairly common occurrence, she experienced a flash of fear. She was in so deep with him, she didn't know what to do with herself. Right when her mind ran off the rails, Darren turned back to her and smiled. Their waitress came by with their drinks and took the rest of their order. The mundane moment brought her back to the present.

When the waitress left, Darren cleared his throat, his eyes sobering. "So, uh, I thought maybe I should talk to you about something."

Risa looked at him carefully. His eyes were slightly guarded. Rather than allowing herself to manufacture anything, she nodded. "Okay."

He took a deep breath and a swallow of beer before speaking again. "I'm sure you've noticed I have nightmares sometimes." At her nod, he continued. "Well, those nightmares are the reason why I didn't date for a long time. Honestly, I didn't plan to ever change that, but then…well you came along." He flushed at this.

She reached over and tugged his free hand into hers, considering whether to tell him Hallie had already told her what happened. He looked determined though, so she elected to let him say what he needed.

He closed his eyes, quiet for a moment. When he opened them again, his gaze was steady. "To make a long story short, I was first on the scene at a car accident in Seattle. It was plain chance I happened to be on the highway so close to where it happened. But I couldn't wait for more help when I got there because one of the cars was smoking so much, I thought it would go up in flames. A little boy was in the back. He was in his car seat, awake and crying. I moved as fast as I could, but it wasn't fast enough. I remember reaching through the window to get him out. Someone called my name and that's the last thing I remember. The car exploded. He didn't survive, and neither did his parents. Though they tell me his parents died from the impact from the accident." He closed his eyes and took a slow breath.

Risa held his hands firmly in hers, stroking her thumb across the back of one of his palms. Darren opened his eyes. They held pain, regret and weariness. Her heart clenched, but she held silent. She'd wanted him to be open with her, and he was. She wasn't going to interrupt.

His voice was gruff when he spoke again. "It took me awhile to pull myself together after that. I was in the hospital for a few days because my lungs were scorched from the heat and smoke from the explosion." He gestured to the faded scar that traveled into his hairline. "I got this when I leaned through the window. Aside from that...well, things weren't good for me for a while. I saw a therapist and he helped. But I didn't know what to do. I knew intellectually it wasn't my fault, but it was still awful. When I was better enough to work again, I decided to come home. Trying to work in Seattle brought up too many memories, and I missed Alaska anyway. Aside from the nightmares, I've been mostly okay. Those are much better than they were. I suppose it'll always weigh on me. But..."

He paused and met her eyes, the raw vulnerability there causing her heart to ache. "I thought I should talk to you about it so you didn't think I was hiding something. Since we're being honest, the truth is I want you more than anyone I've ever wanted. It made me so crazy, I thought I could somehow get you out of my mind by taking a few days with the fire crew. All that did was make me miss you so much it hurt. So, the thing is I haven't been serious with anyone for years. I hate saying it, but I was afraid you'd think something was wrong with me." He cleared his throat, holding her gaze, the intimacy taking her breath away. "But I couldn't bear not to be with you, and it seems like you don't mind my nightmares. They've gotten better lately too. I'm kind of rambling now, but I guess I wanted to make sure you knew how much you meant to me. I can't imagine life without you."

She looked across the table at him and swiped at a tear that tumbled past her lashes. "Oh my. I didn't... didn't expect that."

He shifted his shoulders and flushed. "I needed to be clear where things stood for me. If I had any sense,

I'd have said something sooner instead of getting in my own way."

She took a deep breath, trying to slow her heart down. She needed to make sure he understood how much it meant to her that he'd confided in her. "You didn't have to tell me everything you just did, but it means a lot. I want to be there for you. I get why you might be worried someone would think something was wrong with you, but I never thought that. I tried to be honest yesterday, but I probably didn't clarify that I can't imagine being with anyone but you. So..." She paused for another gulp of air, tears rolling freely down her cheeks. "...it's a relief to know you feel the same way."

Darren's smile was so warm her whole body glowed from within. "Good to know. I take it the tears are a good thing?" His eyes held a glimmer of concern.

She nodded rapidly, snatching the cloth dinner napkin up and wiping her eyes. Their waitress arrived with an appetizer and hesitated when she saw Risa's face.

Risa smiled through her teary eyes. "It's okay. Happy tears."

The waitress smiled and set their appetizer of salmon dip and bread on the table with plates quickly. Dinner passed in a happy blur.

Hours later when she collapsed beside Darren, her skin damp with passion, she tucked her head on his shoulder and sighed. A single lamp cast a golden glow on his chest. She ran her hand across the muscled planes, coasting over the beat of his heart. As her breathing returned to normal, she rolled to her side. "I like your bedroom better."

"How come?"

"Because I love the skylight. I can see the moon, the stars and the snow."

His chest rumbled with his low laugh. "I have an idea."

"What's that?"

He turned his head to look at her. Though she'd just had an earth-shattering orgasm, the heat from his brown gaze set her pulse racing again. "I was thinking maybe Hallie could take over your lease here, and you could stay with me."

A smile bloomed in her heart and spread across her face. "That's brilliant. How soon are you suggesting this happens?"

He smiled softly in the dim light. "As soon as possible?"

Her heart skipped a beat. "Are you sure?"

"Absolutely." He cupped her cheek and brought his lips to hers for a lingering kiss.

Risa waited to turn onto the main road from the gallery parking lot. An eagle flying low along the shoreline caught her eye. She tracked the majestic bird until it came to a slow landing on a piece of driftwood. Distracted, she yelped when her car shifted with a loud thump. Swinging her head around, she looked into the wide eyes of a teenage boy with a mop of brown hair embellished with a purple streak in the bangs. A woman whom Risa presumed to be his mother was shaking her head in the passenger seat.

"You have got to be kidding me," she said aloud to no one since she was in her car alone. She'd been on the way to meet Darren for dinner at the brewery. She quickly texted him, put her car in park and climbed out.

The young man scrambled out of his car, apologizing profusely. "I'm so sorry! I'm learning how to drive stick shift, and I messed up and hit the clutch instead of the brakes."

The woman came around from the passenger side. "Hi there, I'm Gail. Brandon's been doing great with the stick shift, but obviously he's not quite there yet," she said with a wry smile. "Let me get our insurance information." She started to turn away.

"Don't worry about it," Risa said quickly. She gestured to the side of her car. "There's barely a dent. It'll probably be best if I get an estimate and let you know. No need to turn it into more than that."

Gail stopped on her walk back around the car. "Are you sure? I wouldn't ask, but that would be great. I don't know if you have teenage boy, but the insurance rates are insane."

Before Risa could reply, Brandon groaned and hung his head. Risa followed where he'd been looking and saw Darren's patrol car headed in their direction. She looked to Brandon. "Oh, he's not here to give you a ticket. I promise I won't let him give you a ticket, but you should probably be prepared to do some lawn mowing down at the police station for a little while."

Brandon lifted his head, his shaggy brown bangs falling away from his eyes. "Really?" The hopefulness in his question was so endearing, Risa smiled.

"Really. He's my fiancée. He's pretty good at not making something out of nothing. As far as fender benders go, this is close to nothing. Nobody got hurt."

Gail looked worried, but she walked back around the car and stood beside Brandon, threading her arm through his. Darren pulled into the parking lot. When he strolled in their direction, a frisson of awareness ran up her spine, heat suffusing her. It didn't matter that she'd woken in his arms every day for the last year, the mere sight of him set her body alight. His eyes held a gleam. She knew he was amused she'd had another fender bender. Her last car mishap had been with him last year when her engine had overheated, a precursor to the ever-present heat between them.

Darren paused at her side and glanced down at her car, eying the small dent. His chocolate gaze caressed her briefly before he turned to Gail and Brandon. "Hey there Brandon, how's it going?"

Brandon shrugged and shifted on his feet. He kept tossing his head to keep his hair out of his eyes, that streak of purple bouncing each time. "Okay, I guess. I messed up and hit the clutch instead of the brakes and bumped into..." He paused and gestured to Risa.

"Risa," she offered.

"So I bumped into Risa. I'm really sorry." Brandon's face was beet red by the time he finished talking.

Gail jumped in. "Darren, he knows he messed up. Risa here seems to think you won't give him a ticket, but I don't want you to think we expect that from you."

As usual, everyone knew Darren. Risa had grown quite accustomed to that over the year they'd been together. She watched him, warmth pulsing inside. Aside from the fact that he made her body hum, she loved how fair and kind he was. He proceeded to do exactly as she'd expected and offer to let Brandon mow the station lawn in lieu of a ticket. After Gail and Brandon went on their way, Risa turned to him with a grin.

"So do you ever pay someone other than kids to take care of the lawn at the station?"

Darren shook his head. "Of course not! Why would I when there's a constant supply of teenagers making mistakes? I don't let all kids off the hook, but for minor things where no one's hurt and all's well that ends well, I see no reason to be a stickler."

Risa stepped to meet him and tugged him down for a quick kiss. "One of the many reasons I love you," she said against his lips.

He smiled, his eyes dark with heat. "Good thing because I have a long list of reasons why I love you." He pulled back slightly. "So, you just had to go and get in a fender bender two days before our wedding?"

Risa giggled. "Kismet."

* * *

TWO DAYS LATER, Risa stood inside the gallery, her heart so full, she though it might fly out of her chest. A mere hour earlier, she and Darren had been married on the beach. It was late summer. They'd held the ceremony as the sun began its slow descent down the sky, coloring the horizon with soft gold, pink and lavender hues. The mountains were silent witnesses as the waves lapped the shore. Ethan and Jack had organized the reception at the gallery. Food, wine and friends and family were in abundance.

Ethan came to her side, his blue eyes warm. He kissed her on the cheek and tucked his arm into her elbow. "Well dear, you did it. You found a good man and held on. I can't tell you how good it is to see you this happy."

When she looked to him, his eyes were bright with tears, mirroring her own. She swiped at hers. "Don't make me ruin my make-up," she said with a low laugh. Taking a deep breath, she looked around the room, her eyes eventually landing on Darren. He looked devastatingly handsome in his black suit. He'd gamely allowed Ethan and Jack to help him find the suit he wore. She couldn't believe she'd ever thought she could have a fling with him and it would be even close to enough.

She turned back to Ethan. "I should thank you."

Ethan arched a brow in question.

"Because you didn't let me be stupid with him. I was all ready to stand in my own way. *That* would have made me screw up the best thing that's ever happened to me."

Ethan grinned and squeezed her arm. "You deserve nothing less than the best. I only get bossy sometimes, but it was worth it." He loosened his arm from hers and gave her a gentle push. "Get over there. We're about to wind this up. You two have the suite upstairs for the night before you take off tomorrow."

Risa gave him a quick kiss and a whispered thanks before threading her way to Darren's side. They were headed on their honeymoon to the Virgin Islands tomorrow. Ethan and Jack had transformed the upstairs apartment in the gallery into a luxurious suite they rented out for exorbitant rates throughout the summer. Tonight, it was for her and Darren.

Hours later, she leaned against the railing of the balcony overlooking Kachemak Bay. Moonlight shone on the water, rippling in the soft current. She felt Darren's warmth before he slipped his arms around her waist. She wore a thin cotton robe. The heat of his body sifted through the fabric. Her skin prickled with awareness, desire shimmered around them. Stars winked bright in the dark sky.

Darren was quiet. He simply rested his chin on her shoulder, looking out over the water. Their breath rose and fell in unison. The surface of the water broke in the bay. A white gleam flashed in the moonlight, followed by another and another and another. The belugas were back. Risa's heart flew inside. She turned her head, her lips wide with her smile. He met her smile with a soft kiss.

Thank you for reading Tumble Into Love - I hope you loved Risa & Darren's story!

For more swoony small town romance, Travis & Janie's story is next in the Diamond Creek Series in Christmas Nights. Janie is strong, sassy & independent. Travis is all kinds of rugged & sexy, just the kind of man Janie doesn't expect to fall for. Together, they might melt the holiday snow. Don't miss Travis & Janie's story!

Be sure to sign up for my newsletter for the latest news, teasers & more! Click here to sign up: http://jhcroixauthor.com/subscribe/

FIND MY BOOKS

Thank you for reading Tumble Into Love! I hope you enjoyed the story. If so, you can help other readers find my books in a variety of ways.

1) Write a review!

2) Sign up for my newsletter, so you can receive information about upcoming new releases & receive a FREE copy of one of my books: http://jhcroixauthor.com/subscribe/

3) Like and follow my Amazon Author page at https://amazon.com/author/jhcroix

4) Follow me on Bookbub at https://www.bookbub.com/authors/j-h-croix

5) Follow me on Twitter at https://twitter.com/JHCroix

6) Like my Facebook page at https://www.facebook.com/jhcroix

* * *

Visit my store to purchase ebooks & fun swag!

J.H. Croix Shop

Diamond Creek Alaska Novels
When Love Comes
Follow Love
Love Unbroken
Love Untamed
Tumble Into Love
Christmas Nights
Last Frontier Lodge Novels
Take Me Home
Love at Last
Just This Once
Falling Fast
Stay With Me
When We Fall
Hold Me Close
Crazy For You
Just Us
Fireweed Harbor Series
When We Meet - free prequel!
Make You Mine
Dare To Fall - due out June 2023!
Be The One - due out October 2023!
Light My Fire Series
Wild With You
Hold Me Now
Only Ever Us
Fall For Me
Keep Me Close
With Every Breath
All It Takes
Take Me Now - due out August 2023!
Dare With Me Series

Crash Into You
Evers & Afters
Come To Me
Back To Us
Take Me There
After We Fall

Swoon Series

This Crazy Love
Wait For Me
Break My Fall
Truly Madly Mine
Still Go Crazy
If We Dare
Steal My Heart

Into The Fire Series

Burn For Me
Slow Burn
Burn So Bad
Hot Mess
Burn So Good
Sweet Fire
Play With Fire
Melt With You
Burn For You
Crash & Burn
That Snowy Night

Brit Boys Sports Romance

The Play
Big Win
Out Of Bounds
Play Me
Naughty Wish

ACKNOWLEDGMENTS

Every book I write is lifted up by my husband's endless support of my dreams. He's my real-life hero. My editor, Laura Kingsley, continues to make each story better than it was at the start. Many thanks to CT Cover Creations for weaving magic and making my covers beautiful.

Saving the best for last: my readers. Thank you for such fabulous support! Cheers to many more books ahead!

xoxo
JH Croix

ABOUT THE AUTHOR

USA Today Bestselling Author J.H. Croix lives in a small town in Maine with her husband and two spoiled dogs. Croix writes contemporary romance with sassy women and alpha men who aren't afraid to show some emotion. Her love for quirky small-towns and the characters that inhabit them shines through in her writing. Take a walk on the wild side of romance with her bestselling novels!

Places you can find me:
jhcroixauthor.com
jhcroix@jhcroix.com

 facebook.com/jhcroix
instagram.com/jhcroix
bookbub.com/authors/j-h-croix